THE
MISCHIEVOUS
MONKEY CAPER

THE MISCHIEVOUS MONKEY CAPER

•

(Book Seven)
in
The Jennifer Gray Veterinarian Mystery Series

•

GEORGETTE LIVINGSTON

AVALON BOOKS
THOMAS BOUREGY AND COMPANY, INC.
401 LAFAYETTE STREET
NEW YORK, NEW YORK 10003

PRINTED IN THE UNITED STATES OF AMERICA
ON ACID-FREE PAPER
BY HADDON CRAFTSMEN, SCRANTON, PENNSYLVANIA

For Ruth Walker, whose knowledge of the circus was my inspiration. Thanks, Ruthie, and for all your love and support.

Chapter One

With the morning sun warm on her shoulders, and the sweet scent of wildflowers all around her, Jennifer Gray maneuvered Tassie up the slight incline to the stand of peachleaf willows, and looked out over the fertile valley. Fields of corn were already waist-high, and cattle grazed contentedly in the distance. Although there were many places along the equestrian trails around Calico that afforded a rider a place to rest, this spot had always been her favorite because of the incredible view.

From her vantage point, she could also see the large red-and-white-striped tent that had been erected in an empty field northeast of town, prompting a variety of emotions she hadn't expected. There was the excitement, of course, shared by most of the residents in

1

Calico, Nebraska, because The Cannon Family Circus had finally arrived. But she found herself feeling a little melancholy, too. She remembered a day long ago when she had been filled with anger and resentment, and had run off with a circus that was leaving town. She was convinced the happy, lighthearted people in their colorful costumes would provide a much better home for her than her uncompromising grandfather, Wesley Gray, and his stringent housekeeper, Emma Morrison. She hadn't gotten far, only to the next town, before she was discovered hiding in one of the trucks, but instead of punishing her for her misdoings, her grandfather and Emma blamed themselves for not being more understanding. Suddenly, uncompromising became tender, and stringent became compassionate, and what emerged as a result was a little girl who finally felt at home and loved. It wasn't until later that she'd realized she'd been to blame, too, for all those false starts and frustrations during the first few years after her parents' tragic auto accident. Her grandfather had lost his only son, and needed a time for mourning instead of skirmishing with a strong-willed, precocious child who was mad at the world over the loss of her parents. And all poor Emma had been trying to do was hold what was left of the family together. It had been a difficult time for all of them, but by putting their faith in God and pulling together, a strong, unconditional love emerged that had guided her through all those long years of growing up. It continued to guide her later, while she was in college and vet school, struggling to fulfill her dream. Now she was an accredited veterinarian, working as Ben Copeland's assistant at the Front Street veterinary clinic, and the anger she'd felt so long ago was nothing more than a distant memory.

Tassie nickered softly and twitched her ears. Jennifer gave the chestnut mare a loving pat, and smiled. "I know, sweet lady. I heard the whinny, too. Somebody else has decided to take advantage of this extraordinarily beautiful June morning."

Jennifer turned to greet the rider, and was more than surprised to see her grandfather astride Shadow, Max Calder's black gelding. And what a handsome pair they made! Wearing jeans, boots, and a plaid shirt, Wes sat tall in the saddle, and his face, framed by a head of white, wavy hair, was flushed from the ride.

"I thought I'd find you here," Wes said, guiding Shadow up the incline until the two horses stood side by side on the bluff. "I know this is your favorite spot, but I also thought it would be the best place for you to get a good view of the circus. You haven't said, but I have the feeling that having a circus in town again after all these years has stirred up a lot of memories."

Jennifer smiled at him warmly. "Maybe a few, but what I really remember was all your love and understanding. You were my strength even then, and taught me that life really can be wonderful, no matter how many hard knocks we receive along the way."

Wes reached over and patted her hand. "It works both ways, sweetheart. You were my strength, too, in more ways than you'll ever know." He cleared his throat. "Hyde Cannon called about an hour after you left the house. One of the lion cubs is ailing, and he wanted to know if there was a vet in town. Well, I guess you know I was mighty proud to tell him we have two fine vets, and one of them just happens to be my granddaughter. That set him back a bit, but then he still hasn't gotten over the shock of finding out I'm the pastor of Calico Christian Church." Dimples creased his cheeks. "The year his family moved away from Calico, I was a high school linebacker, with a dream of turning pro. Shows you how our lives can turn around, though I never expected him to end up owning a circus, either. He always said he was going to be an actor. Of course, he set me back a bit, too, when he said he does a clown act. His widowed son is managing the circus, and Hyde has a sixteen-year-old grandson who is going to be a lion trainer."

"Sounds like a colorful family. Don't they have a vet traveling with the circus?"

"Just the menagerie boss, who apparently knows a lot about animal care, but can't get to first base with the cub. It won't nurse, and it won't take a bottle. I know this is your day off, but I didn't think you'd mind taking a look at the cub, or care if I tag along. It will give me a chance to visit with my old friend before the hoopla on opening night."

"Of course I don't mind, but if the cub has to be stomach fed, we'll have to go to the clinic first, so I can pick up the tube feeder and formula."

Wes pulled a paper sack out of his saddlebags, handed it to Jennifer, and gave her an impish grin. "I'm way ahead of you. I went to the stable and asked Max for a mount aggressive enough to keep up with Tassie, but gentle enough for an old man who hasn't been on a horse in a year. And then I stopped by the clinic and talked to Ben. He said it sounded like you might have to tube feed the cub, so he put everything you'll need in the bag. He also said for you to be sure and call him if you need help." His blue eyes narrowed in thought as he studied the terrain between the bluff and the circus. Finally, he said, "If we cut through Butler's farm and bypass Muller's Pond, it shouldn't take us any time at all to get to the circus."

"Was Tina at the clinic?" Jennifer asked, leading the way down the trail.

"She was. She was sterilizing surgical packs, and giving Ben a bad time. Actually, she reminds me a lot of you, when you were that age. A bit headstrong, but determined to pursue a career in veterinary medicine. Tina Allen will make a fine vet."

Jennifer smiled. "Yes, she will. It's hard to believe she's been working at the clinic a whole year, or that in another year, she'll be going off to college. We're really going to miss her. By the way, does Emma know you're out gallivanting all over the countryside on horseback?''

"It was her idea," Wes said, pulling Shadow abreast of Tassie as they made their way through a field carpeted with purple lupine and goldenrod. "You mentioned you'd be out riding Tassie most of the morning, so she thought it would save some time if I caught up with you along the trail."

Jennifer said, "She's been so excited about the circus coming to town, I'm surprised she didn't want to come along."

"She thought about it, but she hasn't been on a horse in years, and was afraid she'd slow us down. Of course, she'll want a firsthand accounting the minute we get home. I tried to tell her seeing the circus like this won't hold the same magic it does when all the performers are in their costumes under the spotlights, but that didn't seem to daunt her spirits. She said a circus is a circus, no matter what, and actually admitted to wanting to be a trapeze artist when she was a kid. That's when I admitted I've always had a hankering to be a clown, and that just proves you can live in the same house with somebody for years, and still not know 'em. Every day, I seem to learn something new about that lady, and she never ceases to amaze me."

Jennifer smiled, but didn't comment, because she wasn't about to tell him what she'd suspected for a long time: somewhere along the line, his relationship with Emma had slipped from an affable one into a more affectionate one, and the fun part for Jennifer was wondering what would happen when he finally realized it. Marriage? It was certainly an interesting possibility.

It took fifteen minutes to reach the grassy meadow where the circus was set up, but barely a moment for Jennifer to realize it wasn't what she expected. There was the big top, of course, and a good many smaller tents spread out over the encampment, but the only thing that could even remotely be called a midway consisted of a brightly painted concession stand that sold popcorn, peanuts, hot dogs, cotton candy, sodas, and coffee, a souvenir booth, and a fenced-in ring with a big sign that read, CAMEL AND PONY RIDES FOR THE KIDDIES.

Sensing Jennifer's disappointment, Wes said, "Maybe the show under the big top is so spectacular, Hyde doesn't feel it's necessary to have a midway to bring in business."

Jennifer shook her head. "Maybe, but I was really looking forward to pitching pennies, trying to win a stuffed animal, and going to the sideshow."

Wes pointed at a large, multicolored sign that had been erected on a post that showed a collage of performers and animals. "Well, if we can believe the sign, at least they have a snake charmer. Noya, and her two pythons. Whoa."

Jennifer frowned thoughtfully. "Maybe the circus is in trouble, and that's why there isn't a midway. I mean, when Mr. Cannon called you from Omaha to set this up, he said their next engagement in Des Moines had been canceled, and they weren't due in Topeka until the Fourth of July. I can understand why they had to have a place to stay during the two-week layover, and I can understand why he thought of Calico. It was his hometown after all, they were already in Omaha, which isn't all that far away, and the two of you used to be good friends. But I can't help but wonder why their engagement in Des Moines was canceled."

"I think it's a sign of the times, Jennifer. Circuses are almost a thing of the past, what with the larger ones gobbling up the smaller ones, and from what I've heard, even some of the larger operations have a hard time making ends meet. It isn't difficult to understand when you consider how many people have to be on the payroll to keep things running. Not that I know all the ins and outs, but I can well imagine what it must cost to bring in the stars, or headliners, who in turn draw the crowds. I would think getting rid of the midway would definitely help the overhead. And don't forget, most of the circuses today are held in enclosed arenas. No need for big tops or midways there."

Jennifer sighed. "That's sad, Grandfather, because what's a circus without the big top? And I think everybody in Calico must feel the same way, because from the minute Mayor Attwater and the town council agreed to this, the circus is all they've been talking about. And who can blame them? Calico isn't on the regular circus route, so this is really a treat.''

Before Wes could respond, a tall, thin, angry looking man with black hair and big ears walked out of one of the nearby tents, and his scowl was as quick as his assessment of them. His eyes darted over their jeans, shirts, and boots. ''If you two are lookin' for work, we ain't hiring, so you can just turn yourselves around and skedaddle.''

Annoyed by the man's rude attitude, Jennifer returned, ''My grandfather is a friend of Mr. Cannon's and I'm the vet. Mr. Cannon is expecting us.''

He gave them an aggravated sigh. ''Ah-huh, well, we get all sorts around here, lookin' for work. Well, you'll find Joe Cannon in the one of the menagerie tents out back. You'll see the sign, but you'd better go in waving a white flag, 'cause he's in one of his moods. If you're lookin' for Papa Cannon—that's what we call Hyde—he's in the office.'' He flailed an arm in the general direction. ''It's the silver trailer with the green awning, sittin' beside his motor home. Better go in waving a white flag there, too. *He's* been in a mood for weeks.''

''And you are?'' Jennifer asked.

''Tom Halverson. I'm the head canvasman. That means I'm in charge of putting up and taking down the canvas. Have me a pretty good crew now, even if they are mostly roughies. You towners call 'em roustabouts. Here today, gone tomorrow. Better leave your horses out here, and walk in. Horses don't bother the big cats none, but if Simba decides to let out a roar, your horses might end up tossing you on your ear. I've seen it happen before, just like I've seen towners turn and run when they hear Simba acting up, and think he's on the loose." He gave a quick nod to the right. "You can tether your horses to that hitching post near the kiddie ring. Gideon won't care if you use the space. He won't be exercising the ponies until later this afternoon. But I'd better tell ya, I ain't gonna be responsible for 'em. Got enough to do without worrying about a couple of towners' horses."

After the man stalked off, and they'd tethered the horses, Wes said, "Looks like we should've brought along a couple of white handkerchiefs, if we can believe him, though he's the one who seems to be in a bit of a mood. You go on to the menagerie tent, sweetheart, while I check in with Hyde." He winked at her. "If you run into trouble, scream."

"And if you run into trouble, yell. Shall I come to the office after I'm through with the cub?"

Wes smiled. "You betcha. I can't wait for Hyde to meet my beautiful granddaughter. If you get hung up, I'll find you."

Jennifer gave Wes a hug and, carrying the bag, made her way along the narrow pathway between two tents, stepping over the tangle of wires, cables, and ropes. On the other side, she was confronted with a line of dusty tents, and they all looked alike. There were quite a few workman, or roughies, around doing various jobs, but nobody was smiling, or seemed to care that a stranger was in their midst who might need assistance. Finally, when she found herself going around in circles, she stepped up to one of them and said, "I'm looking for Joe Cannon. He's supposed to be in one of the menagerie tents, and I was told there was a sign—"

The brawny roughie broke in with, "One more row back, lady, but you won't need a sign. Just follow the racket. Goes on day and night. Sometimes I have to put a pillow over my head, just so I can sleep. You want my opinion? They should get rid of all of them, especially the big dude with the big roar."

Jennifer gritted her teeth, and headed for the next row of tents. And by the time she finally found the menagerie tent with the boldly printed sign AUTHOR-IZED PERSONNEL ONLY, KEEP OUT, she was thoroughly convinced there wasn't a friendly person in the circus.

Taking a deep breath, Jennifer walked into the straw-lined tent, waited for her eyes to adjust to the muted lighting, and then made her way through the maze of empty cages and boxes to where two men and a teenage boy stood over a tawny, golden-eyed lioness and her four fuzzy, spotted cubs.

One of the men turned to her and smiled. "You must be the pastor's granddaughter. I'm Joe Cannon."

Embracing his smile after seeing so many sour faces, and a bit breathless because this was the first time she'd seen a lioness and her cubs this close, Jennifer shook his hand. ''I'm Jennifer Gray. I'm sorry it took so long to get here, but this is my day off, and it took a while for my grandfather to catch up with me. He came along, but went to see your father.''

Joe Cannon nodded. ''Good! Maybe seeing an old friend will put a smile on Papa's face.''

''We were given directions out front by a scowling man who said we should come in waving a white flag, because you and your father were in a mood.''

Joe Cannon tossed his head back and laughed. ''You must've met up with Tom Halverson. He's the one who needs an attitude adjustment. As far as he's concerned, the world is a black place, where the sun never shines. Papa and I have our worries, but at least we can appreciate the sun. And a beautiful June day like today. Thanks for coming, Jennifer. My menagerie boss, Beth Tucker, wanted to be here to meet you, but she's come down with some sort of a bug that has given her one whopping headache, and she can't get her head off the pillow. This young man is my son, Mike, and this is Lute Saddler, our lion trainer.''

Mike gave Jennifer a shy, but wide, smile. ''That's trainer, not tamer, like a lot of people think. Lute is teaching me to work with the cats so I can help him in the act.''

"That sounds exciting," Jennifer said, returning his smile. She also made a quick appraisal. Mike Cannon was about sixteen, and had his father's dark hair and pale gray eyes. And like his father, he was tall, thin, and wiry. Lute Saddler, on the other hand, was tall and muscular, and had a head of light blond hair and piercing blue eyes. All three were wearing jeans, flannel shirts, and boots, but she could well imagine what Lute Saddler would look like in full costume, working the cats in the big cage. He would be a headliner all the way.

Jennifer looked down at the exquisite lioness and her cubs, and knew immediately which one was ailing. It was off to one side, wrapped in a towel and barely moving, while its littermates nursed contentedly. "When were they born?" she asked, getting down on her knees.

"Four days ago, before we left Omaha," Mike said. "Zeus was the smallest, and the last born, and he's the only male. Can you help him, Miss Gray?"

Touched by the concern she could hear in the young man's voice, Jennifer gave him an encouraging smile. "I'll sure try, Mike. What are the girls' names?"

"Tania, Sheena, and Delilah," Mike said proudly. "The mother is Pandora, and the father is Simba."

"Was this Pandora's first litter?" Jennifer asked.

"Yes, and it will probably be her last," Joe replied. "She had a tough time, and we thought for a while we might lose her. The whole idea here was to expand our lion population, not put Pandora's life in jeopardy.''

Lute said, ''And heaven knows, it needs to be expanded, what with Sonja and Simba getting on in years—''

Suddenly, a gigantic roar erupted from the other side of the tent, reverberating around them. When Jennifer gasped, Mike grinned. ''That's Simba. He heard Lute say his name.''

''Well, he certainly knows how to make his presence felt!'' Jennifer exclaimed, a little intimidated by the astonishing yowl. She had been about to reach for the cub, but the lioness was watching her intently, making deep, raspy sounds in her throat.

Lute Saddler saw Jennifer hesitate, and chuckled. ''Don't worry about Pandora, Jennifer. I can tell she trusts you.''

Wondering if *she* could trust Pandora, Jennifer quickly examined the lethargic cub. It felt cold in her hands, and the fur was rough and drab, but she could find no other signs of illness, and respiration was normal. ''When did this start?'' she asked finally, tucking the towel around it.

''Early this morning,'' Lute said. ''I took Pandora out for a walk, and when I brought her back, I noticed that Zeus had no interest in nursing. We tried feeding him with a bottle, but he wasn't having any of that, either. I knew right then he was in serious trouble.''

Jennifer said, "I won't say it isn't serious, but he doesn't appear to be ill, in the normal sense of the word. More than likely his small size is prohibiting him from getting the proper nourishment. His litter-mates are much larger, and quite aggressive, and even at this age it's remarkable to watch them tussle for the best position. Have you tried taking away his litter-mates while he's nursing?"

Lute nodded. "That didn't work, either. Didn't show one speck of interest."

"Was he nursing yesterday?"

"Uh-huh, but he didn't show much gusto."

"Then he'll have to be stomach fed, because we'll lose him if he doesn't get some nourishment soon. I thought that might be the case, so I brought along what I'll need."

Joe groaned. "Stomach fed. If you're talking about putting a tube down his throat, that's pretty scary. I saw it done in a vet's office when a poodle in our Canine Follies whelped too many puppies and one of them needed help. The vet said if you get the tube down wrong, milk can get into the lungs and drown the animal."

"Yes, it can, but it really isn't difficult, once you know what you're doing. I'll teach you how to do it, because the cub will have to be fed every two hours."

"Not me," Joe said. "Beth would be much better at that than I would, or maybe Lute. . . ."

At that moment, Simba roared again, though it came out sounding like a yawn. And then there he was, not more than five feet away. Everything about him was magnificent, from his tawny body and dark mane to his majestic stance. Jennifer felt his golden eyes on her as she managed to choke out, "Do you guys know Simba is loose?"

Lute smiled, and snapped his fingers. Immediately the lion ambled to his side, and licked his face with slow, lazy slurps. "Simba is always out of his cage when we're around. He's really a pussycat. Just don't tell anybody."

"And Pandora doesn't mind?"

"Not at all. Lions are a rare breed of cat. The males take right to the cubs, and will even share in their care."

"What about the other cats? Doesn't it bother them to have Simba running around loose?"

"We're keeping the cats in a different tent," Mike said. "Not that we have that many. Just Fang, that's the male tiger, Ember, the black leopard, and Sonja, the old lioness, who barely has a tooth left in her head."

Lute sighed. "Like I said before, our cat population needs a lot of help. . . ."

Lute's words trailed off as a pretty dark-haired woman wearing bright-blue warm-ups ran into the tent and exclaimed, "I can't find Spangle!"

"Did you check to see if she's with Rosie?" Joe asked calmly.

"That was the *first* place I looked." The woman's dark eyes settled on Jennifer. "Guess you must be the vet. Sorry about the interruption, but that wayward monkey of mine is driving me crazy!"

Joe chuckled. "This is Jennifer Gray. Jennifer, Michaela Jones. She and her husband, Gideon, work with the elephants, and own Jammal the camel, six Shetland ponies, a female chimpanzee named Peaches, and Spangle, who is a very creative capuchin monkey."

Jennifer shook the woman's hand. "I don't want to sound totally naive, but what would your monkey be doing in here with the lions?"

Lute grinned and ruffled Simba's mane. "Your question is a logical one, for somebody who doesn't know Spangle. She's made friends with just about every animal in the circus, with the exception of the chimp, the camel, and the poodles. She barely tolerates the chimp, and terrorizes the camel and the poodles every chance she gets. Of course, she also has her favorites. Simba here is one of them, and Rosie the elephant is the other. She rides on Rosie's back during the act, and turns the audience into a frenzy when she plays around under Rosie's big feet. Farrah and Fordel use her in their magic act, too, and occasionally she works with the clowns. Hmm. Maybe she's in Clown Alley, Michaela. Skeetch said something about using her in a new act."

Michaela gave a deep, ragged sigh. ''Well, I'll look there, but if you see her in the meantime, stick her in a cage and lock it!''

After the woman hurried off to find her mischievous monkey, Jennifer turned her attention to the cub, though she still had a smile on her face. The circus, it would seem, was full of surprises, even when the performers weren't in costume and under the spotlight.

Chapter Two

 Because Jennifer thought it would be best to separate the cub from the lioness while she tried to get it stabilized, and not knowing how long it would take, Joe suggested she use his motor home. She would be comfortable there, and have access to his kitchen. Jennifer readily accepted his offer, making sure the cub was wrapped securely in the towel for his journey between the menagerie tent and the area called the "backyard," which was full of motor homes, cabovers, and travel trailers, and looked more like a popular campground than the circus living quarters.

Leaving Mike behind with Lute Saddler to take care to the cats, Joe led the way, pointing out the various trailers and their functions, such as the one used to manufacture ice, the maintenance trailer, and the curious pink travel trailer, festooned with psychedelic wind socks and musical wind chimes.

Joe chuckled when he saw her expression. "That's Beth's trailer. About every other year, she paints it a different color, but no matter what she does, it always ends up dazzling bright. Besides being the menagerie boss, she doubles as the director of Band-Aids, and wants everybody to be able to see her trailer at all times."

"The director of Band-Aids?" Jennifer asked incredulously.

"Yeah. She takes care of all our scrapes, bumps, and bruises, and has part of the trailer set up like an infirmary. We need an aspirin, liniment, or a Band-Aid, we go to her. Anything more serious than that, we go to the nearest town and find a doctor." He waved a hand. "The office is over there, and that's Papa's motor home, sitting beside it."

The office, with its green awning, and Papa Cannon's motor home were set apart from the other trailers, and some distance away. But Jennifer could still see the flower boxes below the windows, and the colorful blooms spilling over the edges. It brought to mind Emma's wonderful flower garden that took up a good deal of space between their little white clapboard house and the church, and it told her a lot about Papa Cannon. He might be living on wheels, but the circus was still his home.

Jennifer was also impressed by Joe's large Winnebago decorated in shades of tan, brown, and cream, but quickly observed that Joe wasn't a very good housekeeper. The small kitchen was littered with dishes, dust was everywhere, and piles of laundry covered the sofa.

"Sorry about the mess," Joe said, scooping up the clothes off the sofa. "Make yourself at home, while I try to find a basket for Zeus."

"A box will do," Jennifer said, choosing a spot on the plaid textured sofa where sunlight spilled through a window.

"No boxes, but this might work," he said, handing her a wicker fruit basket. He shrugged. "We don't have much room, so boxes automatically get tossed out."

Jennifer placed the cub on the towel in the basket, and smiled at Joe. "I don't know that much about motor homes, but I do know every inch of space converts into something else out of necessity, and there is a place for everything, and everything has to be in its place."

"That's about right. That couch you're sitting on converts into a double bed, and the bench behind the kitchen table folds out into a bed. It's just Mike and me, so we manage." He watched Jennifer remove the syringe, tubing, and canned formula from the bag, and visibly shuddered. "You need to warm that up?"

"The formula? Yes, but this is a powder, so by mixing it with warm water, I'll get the right temperature. I'll need a bowl or a jar. . . ."

"Yoo-hoo, it's me," a voice said from the other side of the screen door. The woman opened the door, walked in, and gave Jennifer a warm smile. "I'm Beth Tucker, the menagerie boss, which is just a fancy way of saying I hand out lots of TLC to the animals, and have a strong back. I ran into Mike a few minutes ago, so I knew you were here. I'd shake your hand, but that little bit of jarring would about kill my head. I have this beastly headache that I can't seem to shake, and believe me, I wouldn't wish it on anybody!"

The woman was very pretty, with a head of blond, curly hair, and not even her shapeless coveralls in Day-Glo pink could hide her trim figure. Jennifer liked her immediately. "I'm glad to meet you, Beth. I was hoping we could get together before too long. I'd like to show you how to tube feed the cub, because it's going to be an around-the-clock job."

"I've read about the procedure, and it sounds fascinating," Beth returned, "but maybe I'd better wait, if it means I have to bend over. Just the thought of bending over makes my head pound."

"It can wait until you're feeling better, because I want to get the cub stabilized first anyway," Jennifer said, mixing the formula with warm water in the bowl Joe had provided.

Joe scolded, "I thought you were going to spend the day in bed, Beth."

Beth sighed. "I tried, but I have a bezillion things to do. In case you've forgotten, we open Friday night."

"Everything is under control," Joe returned, "so the only thing you should be worrying about is you. Have you had anything to eat today?"

"It's barely noon, Joe, but if you must know, I had a grape soda and two Oreo cookies. I twisted the cookies apart, and ate the cream centers first. A shrink would probably say I was looking for comfort food like mothers make, but if that were the case, I would've used my last ounce of strength to fix a big bowl of milk toast, floating in butter, cream, and cinnamon. By the way, you're wrong. Everything *isn't* under control. Yolanda and Locke are arguing, Farrah has a rip in her costume, and Gonzo and Skeetch can't agree on the new act." She gave Jennifer a wan smile. "Welcome to The Cannon Family Circus, where anything can happen, and usually does."

Joe groaned. "I left Clown Alley not more than an hour ago, and I thought they had everything settled." He looked at his watch. "Well, they're on their own. I have some paperwork to do in the office that can't wait. I shouldn't be too long, Jennifer, but if you get hungry in the meantime, you'll find sandwich stuff in the fridge, and coffee in the cupboard, if you want to make a pot."

"Tell my grandfather where I am?"

"Will do."

Beth grinned. "I take it your grandfather is that tall, gorgeous, white-haired man I saw earlier, talking to Lani Riggs?"

Jennifer returned, "Well, I don't know Lani Riggs, but the handsome white-haired man *is* my grandfather. He's supposed to be visiting with Papa Cannon."

"He is. When I left, they were sitting in lawn chairs under Papa's awning, drinking tall glasses of Lani's iced tea. Jaffo, Lani's husband, is the cook. He doubles as the sound man during the performances, and Lani waits tables in the cook tent. She's also the circus seamstress. Their daughter, Patty, does makeup and hair, and is engaged to Elijah Shaw, otherwise known as the Pie Man. He's the clown who gets a cream pie in the face at every performance, hence the name."

Jennifer shook her head. "I think it would take weeks for me to sort out everybody. So far, besides Joe, Mike, and Lute, I've only met Michaela Jones, who came into the menagerie tent looking for her wayward monkey."

Beth laughed. "Spangle is something else, that's for sure. She's always been a handful, but since Michaela and Gideon bought Peaches the chimp just before the start of the season, she's been a little terror."

"Sounds like Spangle is jealous. Oh, and I met Tom Halverson."

"Our resident grouch. He's okay, after you get to know him."

A few minutes later, with the syringe full of formula, and the plastic tube attached to the syringe in place of the needle, Jennifer positioned the cub on her lap. Holding the cub firmly, and his head slightly raised, she inserted the tube down his throat. "You'll be all thumbs the first time you try this," she said, smiling at Beth's apprehensive expression. "But it isn't difficult if you gently slide the tube along the back of the tongue. And the most important thing to remember is the feeling of resistance. The tube should go into the stomach smoothly and easily, without forcing it. If you feel opposition of any kind, the tube is probably in the trachea, or windpipe. If that happens, pull out the tube immediately, and try it again.

"Okay, I have the tube in the stomach, and I'm going to depress only a drop. If the cub doesn't choke or cough, it's safe to inject the rest of it. Just remember to do it slowly."

"Is that regular cat formula?" Beth asked.

"Yes, it is. It's much richer in protein and fat than cow's milk. I'll bring along a few extra cans when I check on the cub tomorrow. Oh, and remember to sterilize the syringe and tubing between feedings. Put your fingers on Zeus's belly. You'll be able to feel it fill with milk as I press the plunger."

Beth put her fingers on the cub's belly, and grinned. "That's amazing. How much milk are you giving him?"

"Five CCs for now, because we don't want to bloat his belly. We'll increase that amount in a day or two, and by the end of the first week, he should be getting ten CCs at each feeding. The syringe is marked, and easy to read. He'll have to be fed every two hours for the first few days, but should stabilize out to four feedings a day after that. And hopefully by that time, we can dispense with the tube feedings altogether.

"Beginning tomorrow, he should be taken back to Pandora after each feeding, and be encouraged to nurse. With a little bit of luck, Pandora will accept him. If, by chance, she doesn't, just spread a little butter over Zeus and the other cubs. Mama will lick it off, and regard all the cubs as equal. We use that little trick if we have to place a foundling puppy or kitten with a foster dam or queen. I don't want him left with her though, until he's nursing well and has gained a bit of weight, because it's important to keep him warm, as well as fed. That means while he's away from her, you'll have to be his surrogate mother."

"A job I'll like," Beth said, looking at the cub fondly. "I envy you with all your medical training. I know all the basics when it comes to taking care of the animals, but when it gets down to the nitty-gritty, I have to call in a vet."

"Have you ever thought about becoming a vet?" Jennifer asked, rinsing the syringe and tube in the small, stainless-steel kitchen sink.

''Sure I've thought about it, but I never had the money, or the time. Now it's too late. I'm in my forties, and I couldn't leave the circus for that length of time, even if I wanted to. We don't have a lot of animals, but something is always going on that needs my attention, and—''

At that moment, a tall, dramatic-looking, dark-haired woman, wearing a long, flowing skirt and white peasant blouse, swept through the door and announced, ''Joe said you were here, Beth. Two of the poodles got into a skirmish, and one of them has a nick on the nose.''

Beth rolled her eyes. ''Just like I said. Something is always going on that needs my attention. I'll be back as soon as I can.''

After Beth hurried out, the woman extended her hand. ''I know, you're Jennifer Gray, the vet. I'm Zenobia, ex-fortune-teller, now costume designer.'' She looked in the basket, and shook her head. ''Poor little thing. That litter of cubs means the world to Joe. Means a lot to the circus, for that matter.'' She walked into the kitchen and sighed. ''Not a clean dish anywhere. I swear, that boy gets lazier and lazier. Hmm. Well, maybe you haven't met Mike yet. He's Joe's son, and one big handful.''

''I met him,'' Jennifer said. ''I assume it's Mike's job to wash the dishes?''

''Uh-huh, along with a lot of other stuff he doesn't have time for because all he can think about is working with the big cats. His mama died when he was about seven or eight, and after that taking care of the motor home was a shared responsibility. Real teamwork, with the chores divided up between father and son. Then as time marched on and Papa Cannon's eyesight started to fail, he had to rely more and more on Joe to handle the working end of the circus, so most of the domestic stuff fell on Mike's shoulders.'' She wagged a finger. ''Now, you tell me what's so wrong with that? The days are long gone when girls were supposed to do only 'girl' stuff, and boys were supposed to do only 'boy' stuff. Besides, Joe sees to it Mike gets three meals a day and a roof over his head. And good schooling, too, and all Mike does is complain. And that's something else. Joe and Papa both want him to go to college, and he says no way. He wants to be a famous lion trainer, and says that no amount of schooling is going to teach him that. They've had some pretty big fights about it, when they shouldn't be arguing about it at all. Joe is too easy on him. If he was my kid, I'd sit on his head.''

For all Zenobia's tough talk, Jennifer could hear the concern in her voice. ''I've always wondered about the kids who travel the circus circuit, if that's what it's called. I mean, how do they attend school?''

Zenobia ran hot, soapy water in the sink, and started filling it with dishes. ''Some kids have tutors; some get shipped off to boarding school. Depends how much money the parents have in the bank. In Mike's case, it's easy, and affordable. We have our winter quarters near Sarasota, Florida, and Joe has a good friend who lives nearby. Mike stays with her after we leave in the spring, until school is out, then he goes back and stays with her when school starts in the fall.''

''Then basically, Mike is only with the circus during the summer months.''

Zenobia waved a soapy hand. ''On the road, yeah, though he spends the winter months with us in Florida when we take off our wheels. So you tell me why he can't give a little for a couple of months. He's old enough to see his daddy struggling to keep the circus together, so wouldn't you think he'd want to help?''

''Is the circus in trouble?'' Jennifer said, wanting to chose her words more carefully, but not knowing how.

Zenobia sighed. ''Guess if you're going to spend some time here, things might be easier all the way around if you understand what makes us bunch of oddballs tick. Times are tough, Jennifer. The kids today would rather spend their money at a video arcade than watch a lion jump through a flaming hoop, and their parents are glued to their TVs and VCRs if they want a little recreation. Add to that a tight economy, with everybody trying to hang on to a buck, and business isn't what it used to be.'' She lifted her head proudly. ''We might be a small outfit, compared to some of the others, but we can still give the audience a top-rate performance, no matter how many obstacles get thrown in our way.''

Jennifer picked up a cup towel, and began to dry the dishes. "What kind of obstacles?"

Zenobia frowned. "The kind that can easily give circus people the jitters. You have to understand, people in show business are a superstitious lot, so it's easy to see why there are quite a few of us—and I use the term 'us' loosely because I still don't know what to think—who think this circus is jinxed. Then there are a few who think we might have a crook in our midst. . . . Well, there's no point in getting into that. Anyway, about two years ago, things started happening. Call them accidents, or incidents. Doesn't matter. We had a fire in the cook tent that shouldn't have happened, faulty rigging, sound equipment missing, props busting for no reason, vehicles breaking down, and more recently, we've had some burglaries. Missing jewelry, money, stuff like that."

Jennifer said, "That sounds like a police matter to me."

"No cops. That isn't the way the circus works. If we have a problem, it stays right here. We handle it, and try to work it out ourselves. That doesn't mean if somebody has done something seriously wrong, we won't hand him over to the authorities, but you know what I mean."

"Is it possible somebody is deliberately doing these things, to cause trouble for the circus?"

"Of course it is, and that makes it even worse. It's gotten so bad, everybody suspects everybody, and that's caused a lot of tension. Tempers flare. This might be the lull before the storm, but nothing has happened since we left Omaha, so everybody is afraid to breathe, for fear the other shoe is going to drop.''

''What about security?'' Jennifer asked.

''Just Frank Montano. He does a good job, but he can't be everywhere at once, watching everybody at once. We have a lot of people on the payroll, though if this keeps up, we might lose a few. For example, Gonzo the clown is threatening to leave, and Joveta, who has the Canine Follies, has already talked to somebody from the Baxter and Brown Circus. That's how it happens, how the big guys do in the little guys. The big guys send out scouts. If they see something they like, they make an offer, and it's usually one that's hard to refuse. To tell you the truth, we probably would've lost just about all of our headliners by now if Joe and Papa weren't fair men. They run a good, clean circus, care about their people and the animals, and I'll tell you right now, they don't deserve all the rubbish that's been dumped on their heads.''

They finished the dishes, and while Zenobia poured the coffee she had made into two mugs, Jennifer checked on the cub. Zenobia settled on the sofa and said, ''Give me your hand.''

''Beg pardon?''

''Give me your hand, and let's see what your future holds.'' Jennifer extended her hand, and Zenobia turned it over. ''Ah-ha. You have a nice, long life line.

I also see romance in your future. You have a boy-friend, and he is very tall and handsome.''

Jennifer grinned. ''Yes, he is. His name is Willy Ashton, but he isn't my boyfriend. Well, not exactly. We grew up together, and we're simply good friends.''

''And what does 'not exactly' mean?''

''We date, but we're both much too busy with our careers to get into a serious relationship.''

''Ah-ha. So Willy Ashton is a professional man.''

''He's an attorney, and he's running for mayor.''

''Ah-ha. He's a *successful* professional man.'' She frowned. ''I see sadness surrounding him.''

''That's remarkable, Zenobia. Willy's uncle just passed away. He's in California with his mother for the funeral.''

''Hmm. Well, this little line means you feel a great deal of satisfaction. I think it must have to do with your work. I also see an older woman in your life. A beautiful, vivacious lady, who has influenced you greatly.''

''That must be Emma Morrison. She's been my grandfather's housekeeper for eons, but she's much more than that. She's part of the family, and we adore her.''

''I can also see you are surrounded by many col-orful people. I see a short, portly man. An unscrupu-lous man, who will do anything to get his way.''

''That must be Elmer Dodd. He owns the local dairy, and he's running for mayor, too.''

"And the tall man with the dark hair and eyes, who is associated with the short man?"

Amazed, Jennifer shook her head. "That must be Collin Dodd, Elmer's nephew. He's a displaced vet from Omaha, who has great plans to build a first-class veterinary hospital and put us out of business."

"He won't succeed. Darkness is all around him. I also see a great upheaval, and a river full of water. I believe that's a warning, Jennifer. Take care, and always keep one eye over your shoulder."

"You're really very good, Zenobia. Did you read palms when you were a fortune-teller?"

"Uh-huh, and tarot cards, but my specialty was looking into a crystal ball. You can laugh if you want, but I've always had a gift for seeing into the future. Of course, I did my best work a long time ago, before Papa inherited the circus from Grant Folly. It was the Folly Bros. Circus then. Now, I read palms for my friends, read tarot cards only on special occasions, and gave up my crystal ball for an artist's table."

"Do you design all the costumes for the circus?"

"Uh-huh. And it sure helps to have a good seamstress like Lani Riggs to work with. She whips up my costumes in fine style." She pointed at a line near Jennifer's index finger. "I see mystery and intrigue, too, and it will happen very soon." Her brown, expressive eyes flickered over Jennifer. "You have a question you want to ask me. I can see it in your eyes."

Jennifer flushed. "It's just something you said earlier. Or maybe it's what you didn't say. You said a lot of people think the circus is jinxed, but that some of them think there's a crook among you? I don't want you to think I'm prying, but you've certainly aroused my curiosity."

Zenobia patted Jennifer's hand. "You're an observant young lady. I don't want this to get back to Joe or Papa, even though I'm sure they've heard the rumors. Some of the troupe think Mike is responsible for all the shenanigans. It isn't so far-fetched when you think about it. I mean, Mike's relationship with his daddy and grandpa has been combative at best, and if he really is disturbed, maybe he's trying to strike back."

Remembering the anxiety in Mike's voice when they were discussing the cub's condition, and the genuine concern she could see in his eyes, Jennifer found herself challenging Zenobia's words. "He seems to love the animals, Zenobia. Is it possible such people are overreacting?"

"Of course, it's possible. And I didn't say *everybody* feels that way. Just a handful. But you know what they say—fear breeds fear. If the incidents continue, the rumors will spread, and I'm afraid Mike will eventually get the brunt of it."

"And how do *you* feel, Zenobia?"

Zenobia sighed. "I was with Mike's mama when he was born, and I held Mike's little hand at her funeral.

I held him when he cried, too, and then later, I listened to all his dreams about becoming a famous lion trainer. I watched him grow up into a fine young man who, to my way of thinking, just needs a firmer hand. I guess that tells you I have a hard time believing he would deliberately set out to hurt his daddy and grandpa, or the circus. Still, somebody has to be responsible. And I'm not talking about the accidents, because maybe that's exactly what they were. But the missing jewelry and money is an entirely different matter.''

''Who, in particular, believes Mike is responsible?''

Zenobia's dark eyes narrowed in thought. ''I guess there aren't too many, when you get right down to it. Tom Halverson, the canvasman. He's our Mr. Gloom and Doom, and probably the most superstitious of the whole lot. He's been with Papa a long time, and doesn't think the circus is a place for kids. And then there's Omar. He does the high-wire act, and doesn't like people, period. He sticks to himself, does his job, and collects his pay. Tawno thinks it's Mike, too. She's our only lady clown. Tawno means 'tiny' in Gypsy. She isn't a midget, but she's a little slip of a thing, with a head of silver hair and a figure to die for. She came from the Sarazan Circus with Locke Leone, who's the other half of our equestrian team, and they're romantically involved. Locke thinks Mike is the culprit, too, though he isn't as vocal about it.''

''Who is the other half of the equestrian team?''

"Yolanda, and she can't stand Tawno. Not that she has eyes for Locke or anything, but there is a definite personality clash. Of course, she doesn't get along with Locke, either. Oh, and Anthony Franzenie has made some noise in that direction. He's part of the Flying Franzenies. Two brothers and a sister. If anybody else is thinking it, they're keeping their thoughts to themselves."

"Do you know who started the rumor?" Jennifer asked.

"That would be pretty hard to pinpoint. You know how it goes. Somebody says, 'I heard this or that,' and you never find out where they heard it. Reminds me of a game I used to play when I was a kid. You know. You sit in a circle, and whisper a little story in your next-door neighbor's ear, and that person passes it on. By the time the story gets all the way around the circle, it's blown totally out of proportion." Her face broke into a smile, and she patted Jennifer's hand again. "For what it's worth, I think we have a pretty good group of people working for the circus, and we'll get to the bottom of it, sooner or later. And who knows. Maybe coming to Calico for this two-week layover will bring us luck." She closed her eyes, and waved a hand dramatically. "This seer of great magic hears footsteps, and the jangle of coins. Prepare yourself. You're about to meet Spangle."

Seconds later, Beth walked in, carrying the most adorable little monkey Jennifer had ever seen. "This is Spangle," Beth said, blowing at a stray wisp of hair that had fallen over her forehead. "I found her terrorizing the poodles, and now I can't find Michaela. Lute said Michaela wanted her locked in a cage if anybody found her, but I simply couldn't do it. Though if she doesn't behave . . . Spangle, stop that!"

Spangle was about a foot and a half long with a slim prehensile tail, and was nearly all black, but for the white face and white cape pattern across her back and shoulders. Even if she hadn't been told, Jennifer would have known Spangle was a capuchin monkey by the black cowl on her head, resembling the habit of the Capuchin monks. She was typically an organ grinder's monkey, a species loved worldwide and known for its charm and intelligence. At the moment, Spangle had her long arms wrapped around Beth's neck, and was covering her face with smacking kisses. But her dark, wonderful eyes were on Jennifer. She was obviously showing off.

Jennifer stepped closer, and put out a hand. "Hello, Spangle. You are a sweetie. And will you just look at that pretty coin necklace, and fancy red apron!"

Trying to disengage the monkey's arms from around her neck, Beth said, "Spangle has a whole wardrobe of pinafores with pockets, though when she's in an act, she wears sparkles and spangles."

Jennifer winked at the monkey. "Well, now I know how you got your name." Spangle reached out and

took Jennifer's hand, and she was amazed by the soft-
ness of the monkey's paw.

"Uh-huh, but a lot of people call her 'Jangles'. The
necklace has become her trademark. Michaela put it
around her neck so she could keep track of her, but a
lot of good it did. She's a sly one, especially if she
doesn't want to be seen or heard.''

Zenobia got up and stretched. "Well, I'll leave you
two to the cub and Spangle. Lunch should be about
over in the cook tent, and I have to help Lani with the
costumes. If you'd like a good cup of coffee, Jennifer,
stop by my trailer anytime. It's the little white one
near the cook tent that's hooked up to a rickety brown
truck.''

"She's a neat lady,'' Jennifer said after Zenobia had
gone.

Beth replied, "Yes, she is, and she's got a heart as
big as the ocean. Speaking of lunch, that handsome
grandfather of yours said to tell you Papa is expecting
you for lunch. I'll baby-sit Zeus and Spangle, so you
go ahead and have a good time.''

"But what about your headache?''

"It's better, honest. In fact I feel so much better, I
should be able to try my hand at the next tube feeding.
Oh, and if you happen to see Michaela, tell her I have
Spangle. And tell her not to worry. I'll take good care
of her. For all my complaining, I do love the little
rascal.''

Spangle was making low chattering sounds in her throat, and had lovingly placed her head against Beth's shoulder. "If I see her, I'll tell her," Jennifer said, walking out into the bright sunlight, and feeling its warmth all the way to her heart.

Chapter Three

Jennifer found her grandfather and Papa Cannon sitting in white webbed lawn chairs under the green awning, enjoying their camaraderie and a pitcher of iced tea. And for the first time, she realized why Papa had claimed this section of the "backyard" as his own. It was on a little rise, for one thing, affording him a splendid view of the encampment and the countryside beyond, and the ground was carpeted with clover. Several small lawn tables were scattered about, and the one closest to Papa's chair held an assortment of folders and papers.

"Ah, here you are," Wes said, standing up to give Jennifer a hug. "When Hyde suggested you join us for lunch, I told him you might not want to leave the cub."

"Everything seems to be under control," Jennifer said, returning his hug. "Beth is baby-sitting, and the next feeding isn't until two." She turned and smiled at the gray-haired man as he pulled his tall, lanky frame out of the chair. He, too, was wearing boots and western-style apparel, but what struck her the most was how much he resembled Joe and Mike. "Hello, Mr. Cannon. It's nice to finally meet you."

Papa shook her hand, and gave her a lopsided grin. "Call me Papa. Everybody does. Well, now, your grandpa said you were pretty, but he didn't tell me you had lion-colored hair." He squinted, and stepped closer. "And blue eyes. 'Bout the color of bluebells." He waved a hand. "I'd have me some bluebells in those flower boxes, but this is the wrong time of year. Best I can do is what you see, marigolds and pansies. Your grandpa was telling me he grows vegetables at home, and that the lady of the house grows flowers."

Taken back for a moment, until she realized he was talking about Emma, Jennifer nodded, but gave Wes a sly glance. "And the lady of the house argues with him all the time about who grows the best this or that, which is rather like comparing apples and oranges. I mean, how can you compare a tomato to a snap-dragon?"

A flush had touched Wes's cheeks. "Ah, well, I told Hyde all about Emma, sweetheart, and how she's been taking care of us for a good long time."

Papa said, ''And from the looks of you two, I'd say she's doing a good job. But let me tell you, Jennifer, your grandpa has sure changed. Back in our school days, his hair was dark brown. He was on the lean side, too, though he always did have a set of shoulders and arms.''

Wes smiled. ''You've changed, too, Hyde. You weren't nearly as tall and, as I recall, you would've rather jumped off the White River Bridge than wear cowboy boots and jeans. I remember you saying that actors were supposed to look like actors offstage, too, so you wore your Sunday clothes, seven days a week.'' He winked at Jennifer. ''In today's jargon, I think it's called being a nerd.''

Papa's grin widened. ''Just shows you how things can change. Speaking of good jobs, Jennifer, I think you are doing a fine one. Joe said you think the cub is going to pull through. That litter of cubs means a lot to the circus, and after almost losing Pandora, well, I want to thank you, from the bottom of my heart.''

Warmed by his words, Jennifer gave him an encouraging smile. ''I can't make any promises, but I think with the proper nourishment and the chance to catch up with his littermates, Zeus is going to be just fine. I'll stay for the next couple of feedings, and by then, Beth should be able to take over, though I do plan on coming by each day to check on him.'' She handed Papa her card. ''Ben Copeland's number is

listed, too. He's my colleague at the Front Street animal clinic, and he's a terrific vet. You can call us day
or night if you run into any problems.''

Papa gave a relieved sigh, and nodded. ''Sit a spell,
Jennifer, and have some iced tea. Lunch should be
along in a few minutes. Patty is bringing us a plate of
sandwiches from the cook tent.''

Jennifer poured iced tea into a tall glass, and said,
''Patty is Lani and Jaffo's daughter, right?''

Papa nodded. ''So, you've met our Patty.''

''No, as a matter of fact, I haven't, but Beth told
me all about her, and about her family. Jaffo is the
cook, but doubles as your sound man, and Lani is a
waitress in the cook tent.''

''Did Beth tell you that Lani is also our seamstress?''

''Zenobia told me.''

''You met Zenobia already, huh?'' Papa said.
''Well, I guess that means you know more about the
circus than I do.''

Jennifer smiled. ''Is that a polite way of saying she
likes to talk?''

''Talk, gab, gossip, call it what you want. She
joined the circus years ago, and she hasn't stopped
jabbering since. Don't get me wrong. Zenobia is one
fine lady, and I don't know what we'd do without her.
And we all have our shortcomings. Hers happens to
be the gift of gab. She tell your fortune?''

''Yes, she did, and it was really quite remarkable.

But then, she's a remarkable lady. And the animals! They're wonderful!''

Wes's eyes twinkled. "Like Spangle? When Beth Tucker stopped by earlier, that little monkey was doing handstands, showing off. She managed to charm me, that's for sure.''

Jennifer returned, "Isn't she amazing? Oh, and wait until you meet Simba. He's the cubs' daddy, and is truly magnificent.''

"Did he lick your face?'' Papa said with a chuckle.

"No, but he licked Lute's face.''

Wes rolled his eyes. "Lute. That's a new name. With so many animals and performers, I don't know how anybody can keep track of the players without a program.''

"Don't see where it would be much different than memorizing all the names in your congregation,'' Papa said, picking up a folder off the table. He pulled out a long sheet of paper, and handed it to Wes. "But this might help. It's a roster. Joe has been working on it for a couple of days, shuffling acts around. Gotta keep everybody happy. What you see there is the way it will go, barring any calamities.''

The sheet of paper looked like a family tree, and Jennifer studied it over Wes's shoulder.

RINGMASTER: Joe Cannon

WALKAROUND: Led by Jammal the camel

RING ONE:
Clowns
Rope Act
Pythons

CENTER RING:
High Wire
Equestrian
Elephants
Trapeze
Big Cats

RING THREE:
Papa
Canine Follies
Magic Act
Clowns

Encores, depending on time and size of audience

CLOWNS: The Pie Man, Skeetch, Tawno, Gonzo, and Papa
EQUESTRIAN: Locke and Yolanda
ELEPHANTS: Gideon and Michaela—Rosie, Boris, and Yogi
CANINE FOLLIES: Joveta
PYTHONS: Noya
MAGIC ACT: Farrah and Fordel
ROPE ACT: Farrah and Fordel
HIGH WIRE: Omar
THE FLYING FRANZENIES: Nichole, Arturo, and Anthony
BIG CATS: Lute with Simba, Fang, and Ember. Mike on cage.

Note: Spangle will work with the elephants and the magic act.

"I see Farrah and Fordel do the rope act and the magic act back-to-back." Jennifer said. "That must be really hard."

Papa frowned, and squinted at the paper. "That's not the way it's supposed to be. I used to take care of all this stuff before my eyesight started failing. Not that I'm blind or anything, but words and numbers can be pretty fuzzy."

"Don't you wear glasses?" Jennifer asked.

He shook his head. "Wouldn't do any good. Got cataracts in both eyes."

"Have you ever thought about having surgery? They do a remarkable laser surgery now, and—"

Papa interrupted with a wave of his hand. "No way. I haven't got the money, the time, or the inclination. Haven't seen the inside of a hospital since I had my tonsils out, and that was when I was a tadpole and didn't know any better."

"What does 'Mike on cage' mean?" Wes asked.

"Means he'll be in the ring working the cage doors for Lute. We have cage men who work behind the scenes, but putting the boy in the ring like that gives him the experience of being in front of an audience. Someday, he'll make a fine lion trainer." He looked at Jennifer and gave her a wan smile. "I suppose Zenobia told you all about the battle of wills that's going on?"

"You mean about Mike going to college? Yes, she did."

"Someday, he'll inherit the circus, and when that time comes, he should have a good, solid education behind him, instead of having to learn everything the hard way, like I did. Joe sees it a different way. He says in a few years, there won't be any circuses, so Mike should plan for the future in a different direction. I say that's a bunch of baloney. Circuses have been around forever, and they are *gonna* be around forever. It might be tough going along the way, but like anything else, things that count shouldn't come easy, if they're gonna have any meaning. Hard work and determination. That's what it takes.''

"Mike is only sixteen," Jennifer reminded him. "So he has some time to change his mind, and he may do you proud yet. Sometimes, it's hard to remember what it was like to be sixteen. It's a wonderful age, but it can also be a little overwhelming. You're so close to being an adult, yet you're tired of school and want to get on with your life. Therefore, you have a tendency to want to jump from point A to point C, bypassing B. Mike seems like a very nice young man, and I'm sure he'll come around with time."

"Maybe, maybe not, but giving him time is the way I feel about it, too. Joe is too hard on him, and around and around they go. 'Course, Zenobia probably told you she thinks Joe is too easy on him, but we're talking about two different things here. One has to do with him going off to college and getting a good education, and the other has to do with his chores around the circus. Me? I think the boy is pretty normal in that respect. You tell him to wash the dishes, or dust the furniture, and he'll come up with a dozen different excuses why he can't or doesn't have the time. But you ask him to clean out the menagerie tent, hose off the elephants, pitch hay, or muck out the horse stalls, and he'll be right there with a smile on his face. 'Course, these days, you won't see too many smiles around the circus. Knowing Zenobia, I'm sure she told you about all our mishaps, and what some of the folks are saying. Well, I say, whoever thinks the circus is jinxed, can just move on. I say, we've had a run of bad luck, and like I told your grandpa, what goes around, comes around. We'll get through it, and we'll move ahead. With or without the dissenters.''

Wes handed the roster back to Papa. ''You're listed with the clowns, Hyde. Does that mean you are a part of the clown acts?''

Papa glanced at the roster, and placed it on the table. ''No way. I started my solo act years ago. It worked then, and it works now, no matter what Joe says. He wants me to retire my act. He says my timing is off, and one of these days I'm gonna get hurt. I keep telling him I could do that act blindfolded, but he won't listen. 'Course, if anything ever happens to Sassy Dancer, I might be in a bit of a bind. She's a noble Andalusian, and as smart as a whip. She knows how I think, and I know what she's thinking, and that's why we make a good team.'' He looked off across the field, and squinted. ''That must be Patty heading up the hill. Brown hair and wearing bib overalls?''

''Yes,'' Jennifer said, ''and she's carrying a tray.''

At that moment, Joe stepped out of the silver trailer, took a deep breath, and ran a hand through his dark hair. He looked disheveled and troubled, but he managed to give Jennifer a smile. "The fact you're here must mean the cub is better," he said, pulling up a chair.

Before Jennifer could respond, Patty Riggs arrived with the tray of sandwiches, and her words bubbled over. "Sorry it took so long, but I couldn't get away from Zenobia. All she could talk about was Jennifer." She put out a hand. "And you must be Jennifer. I'm Patty Riggs. If the sandwiches aren't edible, it's my fault. I'm not too good in the kitchen, but my dad was busy, and my mom is knee-deep in costumes."

Jennifer caught the curious frown on Joe's face before she shook Patty's hand. "The sandwiches look delicious, Patty. Will you join us?"

"Can't. Michaela's costume is about finished, and it needs to be fitted, but nobody can find her, so I have to stand in." She shook Wes's hand. "You must be Pastor Gray. Well, sorry this is 'hi' and 'good-bye.' Maybe I'll see you later?"

Wes shook his head. "I have a meeting this afternoon, so I have to get back to town."

Jennifer said, "I'll be here until around four. I'd stay later, but we came on horseback, and want to get back to the stable before dark."

Patty winked at Joe. "If she knows all about horses, maybe you should hire her for the equestrian act, and give Yolanda a run for her money. Bye-bye."

After Patty had gone, and everybody had helped themselves to a sandwich, Joe said to Jennifer, "How did you meet Zenobia?"

He was still frowning, and his words were stiff. Was he upset because she'd talked to Zenobia? "She came by your motor home after you left," Jennifer said lightly. "She's a very nice lady."

"And did she give you the history of the circus?"

"She told me a little bit about circus life, but I don't think you could consider it giving me 'the history of the circus.' "

Oblivious to his son's rankled attitude, or choosing to ignore it, Papa gobbled up a sandwich, and pointed at the roster. "Says there that Farrah and Fordel are doing their acts back-to-back."

"Yes," Joe replied, "because Joveta refuses to work with the Canine Follies. She says the poodles' barking upsets the pythons. She was so distressed, Farrah and Fordel offered to change places with her for the rope act. The clowns are skirmishing too, so I'm not sure what will come of that." He finally smiled at his father. "But you know how it is when it gets this close to opening night."

Papa said easily, "Things are bound to get a little testy." He reached over and patted Jennifer's hand. "But don't you worry, young lady. We're gonna give the old hometown a show to remember. Want you and Wes and that lady of the house, along with all your friends, to come to the party after the show, too. Always have a little get-together in the big top after opening night, and most folks enjoy it. It's a way for folks to meet the performers up close, and ask all those questions they are always dying to ask.''

"It's called P.R.," Joe said, getting to his feet. He looked at his watch. "Sorry to have to run, but I'd better check on things in Clown Alley."

Jennifer stood up as well. "And I have to sterilize the syringe and tubing before the next feeding. I'll probably see you later, Papa, and I'll see you at home," she said, kissing Wes's cheek.

Joe had already reached the maintenance trailer when Jennifer caught up with him. "Can I talk to you for a minute?" she said, trying to catch her breath.

Joe turned, and gave her an indifferent shrug. "That's what I've got. Just about a minute."

Trying to ignore the impatience in his voice, Jennifer said, "I've been wondering how to approach this, but I've never been one to mince words, so I'll just say it. I get the feeling you're unhappy with me. Is it because I talked to Zenobia?"

Joe sighed. "It isn't you, Jennifer. It's Zenobia. She has the tendency to tell tales out of school, if you'll excuse the cliché, and because of it, a lot of facts can get distorted."

"You mean like all the misfortunes that have been happening to the circus?"

"That's only part of it, though I would suspect most of what she told you is true. Did she tell you anything else?"

"I don't want to get her in trouble, Joe. . . ."

"There is no such thing as getting Zenobia into trouble, and that's the problem. She's simply Zenobia, and her love for gossip goes with her personality."

"Then you must know she told me about the certain few who believe Mike is responsible for all the mishaps."

"I figured as much, so I guess my question to you is, did you mention it to my dad?"

"No, I didn't. Is that what you've been worried about?"

Joe kicked at a pebble, and stuffed his hands into the front pockets of his jeans. "You have no idea how hard I've tried to keep those rumors from getting back to him. Just like I've kept the overdue bills away from him, along with most of the hassles among the discontents. Papa is getting on in years, and shouldn't have to spend the time he has left, worrying and fretting."

"You make it sound like he's going to drop dead tomorrow," Jennifer said indignantly.

"I'm sorry if that's the way it sounded, but facts are facts. He isn't as strong as he used to be, and then with his failing eyesight—"

Jennifer broke in, "He looks pretty strong to me, physically and mentally, and his eyesight could be greatly improved if he would have cataract surgery."

"And did he also tell you he'd rather drink poison than set one foot in a hospital?"

Jennifer smiled. "In so many words. I know he can probably be a very difficult man at times, but I don't see where being overprotective can be all that beneficial. And if you want my opinion, I think he knows a lot more than he lets on." She reached out and touched his arm. "I'm sorry, Joe. I know I'm way out of line here, but I live with my grandfather, who is about your dad's age, and I wouldn't dream of keeping secrets from him. And believe me, I embrace his love and wisdom."

Joe's face softened. "I'm sure you do, but I wonder how you'd feel if your grandfather was running around the circus ring, trying to catch up with his horse, and before he does, he falls at least a dozen times. Or how you'd feel if you watched your grandfather throw all the bills in a box, and casually say, 'We'll toss 'em all up to the ceiling, and whatever one sticks, we'll pay.' Or if you knew your grandfather spent hours every night pacing the floor, and worrying himself sick. Papa might talk a good game, but inside he's hurting plenty. How can I add to that, by dumping all the problems on his shoulders?"

"Does Mike know about the rumors?" Jennifer asked.

"I haven't talked to him about it, if that's what you mean. But even if he does, he's probably ignoring them. He's good at ignoring everything. He lives in his own little world, Jennifer, and that world basically includes Lute and the cats. I call it tunnel vision. I'd like nothing more than to be able to snap my fingers and have a miracle cure for all our problems, but I can't. So I muddle along, keep my fingers crossed, say a lot of prayers, and hope we can get to the end of each season somewhat intact. But no matter what, I'm glad we came to Calico. We haven't had any incidents since we left Omaha, for one thing, and like I said earlier, seeing your grandfather has put a smile on Papa's face. And seeing your pretty smile has helped me. If you'll join me for supper in the cook tent tonight, I'll make sure Jaffo adds extra Parmesan to the pot of spaghetti.''

''That's very sweet, Joe, but I'll be leaving about four. Beth should be able to handle things by then, and your dad has my card and phone number, if anybody needs me later tonight. But I'll see you tomorrow, when I stop by to see the cub.''

''Until tomorrow then,'' Joe said, walking off.

Jennifer swallowed around the lump in her throat. She, too, would say a few prayers for The Cannon Family Circus, and for a speedy end to all their problems.

It was almost six when Jennifer made her way along the tree-lined pathway between the church and the house, and so much had happened over the course of the day, it seemed she'd been gone for weeks. The sun, like a crimson lantern hanging low in the sky, cast its last warm rays over the garden, where her grandfather's vegetables were finally poking up through the rich, sandy soil. Emma had gotten an earlier start with her flowers, and it wouldn't be long before they would have a colorful display, and the sweet scent of them would fill the air.

She smiled, thinking about Papa Cannon's little window-box gardens as she made her way into the house, and all the other touches he had added to make his living quarters a real home. And it only took her a moment to realize Emma and her grandfather were bickering. Debating this issue or that had become a habit for them over the years, but lately, it seemed their heated words were spoken in a lighter manner, and much more playfully. She could also smell chicken soup, and her grandfather *hated* chicken soup. He claimed the only thing it was good for was a cold, and even then he had to be nearly delirious with a fever before he would attempt to choke it down.

"I don't care if you had a late lunch," Emma was saying as Jennifer walked into the cozy, yellow kitchen. "That was almost five hours ago, and you've been sneezing ever since you got home. You say it's allergies, and I say it's the beginning of a summer cold, but either way, you'd feel a lot better if you eat a bowl of soup."

Wes held up a hand and scowled. "You hear that, Jennifer? She admits she's trying to poison me with that concoction she's got bubbling on the stove."

Emma pushed a strand of brown, wiry hair from her forehead with the back of her hand, and said, "I never said any such thing! And that's all *he* knows, Jennifer. He might be one of the smartest men alive, but when he comes to his health, it's like his brains took a trip and left him behind."

Jennifer gave Emma a hug, and leaned over to kiss Wes's cheek. "I'm sorry you aren't feeling well, Grandfather, but I'm just too tired to take sides." She dropped to a chair and kicked off her boots. "Must be in the air. Beth Tucker has had a headache off and on all day, and when I left her, she was in the middle of a sneezing fit."

"Allergies," Wes announced. "Could be all the circus hay, the straw, the tanbark, sawdust, or maybe it's the goldenrod that's in full bloom. Must've been all that rain we had a few weeks ago that stirred things up. I remember one year when all of Nebraska was so deep in pollen, it turned the sky yellow."

Emma shook her head. "Your granddaddy is also the biggest teaser east of the Divide."

Jennifer said, "I'll attest to that, though Papa Cannon comes in a close second. I stopped by to see him before I left the circus, and he was in a frisky mood. He even put on the red wig he wears in his act, and tried to tell me it was made from the wool of some rare, Tibetan yak, instead of everyday yarn."

Wes grinned. "I take it the cub is doing better?"

"The cub is doing fine, Grandfather. After just two tube feedings, he began to rally. I wasn't going to put him back with Pandora until tomorrow, but we gave it a try after the last feeding, and it was quite remarkable to see him rooting and scooting around. Even better, the lioness was showing a great deal of interest in him. He still wasn't nursing when I left, but I think it's only a matter of time. Because Beth wasn't feeling all that well, I thought I'd better teach Lute Saddler how to tube feed the cub, too. That way they can alternate feedings during the night."

"Lute Saddler, the lion trainer?" Wes asked.

"Right."

"So how did he do?"

"Fantastic, but then Lute has a way with the cats that you'll just have to see to believe."

Emma shivered. "I told your granddaddy where there is a lion cub, there has to be a mama lion. And I don't care if the mama belongs to the circus. A lion is a wild animal, and unpredictable, and—"

Wes broke in with, "Oh, Emma, Jennifer came home with all her fingers and toes, and I don't even see a scratch." He winked at Jennifer. "From what I heard, the mama is a pussycat, and even eats out of the trainer's hand."

"Well, almost. Pandora is very tame, and Simba—well, you'll see for yourselves tomorrow night."

Emma frowned. "And I suppose Simba is the papa?"

"That's right, and he's a pussycat, too, though you wouldn't know it when Lute puts him through his paces. He's done an incredible job turning a pussycat into a ferocious beast for the benefit of the act. And the best part is, he does it with love. And just wait until you meet Spangle!"

"Your granddaddy told me all about Spangle, and I'll admit, a small monkey is much more to my liking. Even if she is mischievous." Emma's eyes twinkled. "Guess I'd better admit something else, too. I can't wait for Friday night!"

"I'm excited, too," Jennifer said. "Especially after I caught a little of the dress rehearsal."

Emma rolled her eyes at Wes. "It sounds like Jennifer did a lot more than take care of a lion cub. So, are you still full of ham sandwiches? Or would you like a bowl of soup?"

"A bowl of soup sounds wonderful, Emma. And while I eat, I'm going to tell you all about The Cannon Family Circus, and then you tell me, because something is definitely amiss."

Wes said, "Uh-oh. Something tells me we have another mystery in the making. Does this have anything to do with all the mishaps Hyde was talking about?"

"Yes, it does, and I don't know if it's exactly a mystery, but it's certainly thought-provoking."

For the next hour, Jennifer told Wes and Emma what she knew, adding a few of her own observations, and by the time she was through, Wes had forgotten about his allergies, and Emma had nearly let the soup boil dry on the stove.

Realizing what she had done, Emma rushed to turn off the burner, and exclaimed, "Lordy, if that isn't the ticket!"

Wes gave her a roguish grin. "Your loss is my gain, Emma. Now if you really want to make me happy, you can bring out that strawberry pie you've got hiding in the pantry."

"Yum," Jennifer said. "I'd like a piece of that, too, Emma."

Emma muttered something about being outnumbered, and headed for the pantry.

A few minutes later, with thick wedges of strawberry pie in front of them, Wes said, "So you really think somebody is trying to sabotage the circus?"

"Everything points in that direction, Grandfather. At first, I thought it might be another circus. You know, big circus wants little circus, little circus refuses to sell, so big circus resorts to using underhanded tactics. But Joe said nobody has made them an offer in years."

"Maybe it's a disgruntled performer, or somebody else who works for the circus."

"Well, I would rather believe that than believe Mike is responsible. I'm told he's moody at times, strong-willed, and can even be a bit defiant, but he seems like a good kid, and I don't think he would do anything to hurt his family or the circus."

"So maybe the accidents are just accidents," Wes said thoughtfully. "Maybe they've simply had a string of bad luck, and that can happen to anybody, in any business. And when you add in the fact that circus people are renowned for being superstitious, well, it probably wouldn't take much to stir things up."

"I agree, but don't forget they've had a recent rash of burglaries. And the latest incident—Oh, you don't know about that. It happened after you left. If you'll recall, nobody could find Michaela."

"Spangle's owner? I remember. That nice girl, Patty, said Michaela's costume was ready to be fitted, but nobody could find her."

"That's right. Well, Michaela turned up about three o'clock, terribly upset, and jabbering in Italian. Joe finally got her calmed down enough to tell us what happened. Earlier, Spangle disappeared, which she frequently does, and Michaela looked for her everywhere, including the secluded area behind the circus where they keep the elephants tethered, because Spangle and Rosie, the elephant, are good friends. Well, when she went back to the elephant area a second time, Rosie was gone. Michaela should have called for help right then, but she wasn't thinking. She just jumped in one of the little electric carts they use to scoot around the encampment, and took off on her own. She finally found Rosie down near Willow Creek, and led her back to the circus."

"I can't believe somebody didn't notice the elephant was missing," Emma said.

"I know, but things get a little crazy this close to opening night, with everybody scrambling around with a million things to do. Gideon, the bull man, who is also Michaela's husband, was out front exercising the ponies, and nobody saw Michaela take off in the cart, either, if you can believe it. Now comes the scary part."

"Boy oh boy," Wes said, taking a deep breath.

"That's right, boy oh boy. Each elephant wears a bracelet around an ankle, and each bracelet has a loop. A rope goes through the loop, and is attached to a stake that goes into the ground. I know that doesn't sound like much to hold an elephant, but all three are wonderfully docile, and would never run off, under normal circumstances. Well, somebody cut the rope, and must have goaded Rosie on with some sort of prod, because they found several wounds on her flank. They weren't deep, but it was enough to upset her, and send her off on a run. And from what I understand, elephants can really run. Thank goodness Michaela went back to check the elephant area a second time, or Rosie would probably be in Cherry County by now."

Emma shook her head sadly. "That's terrible, and frightening."

"Does everybody know what happened?" Wes asked.

"No. Just Joe, Beth, Michaela, Gideon, Lute, and Mike, and that's the way Joe wants to keep it. Oh, and Frank Montano. He's the security guard. But he's only one man, and can't be everywhere at once."

Wes said, "I'm surprised they didn't hire additional guards when the trouble started two years ago."

"None of it seemed serious enough to justify the added cost, I would imagine, but now they might have to, even though they can barely meet expenses."

"Sounds to me like they should keep the percentage of the receipts they plan on turning over to the town," Emma said.

"Papa Cannon is a proud man, and wants to pay his way," Wes said. "When we set this up, I told him the town council agreed he could use the land for the two-week layover without charge, but he wouldn't hear of it. He said the circus would put on three performances while they were here, and give a percentage of the receipts to the town. And it wasn't open for discussion."

"Maybe they should call the sheriff," Emma said thoughtfully.

Jennifer said, "I suggested it, but that wasn't open for discussion, either. Circus people live in a closed group, and prefer to keep their problems to themselves."

Emma clucked her tongue. "Well, they asked for your help, didn't they?"

"Yes, but that's different, Emma. The animals mean everything to them, so I'm sure if they could afford it, they would hire a resident vet. Beth comes close, but she has her limitations."

Wes's eyes narrowed in thought. "You didn't mention Hyde when you listed the people who know about the elephant incident, sweetheart."

"Joe made the decision not to tell him. I'll admit that upset me, because I think Papa is kept in the dark entirely too much, but then when I stopped by to see him before I left the circus, and he was in that wonderful, teasing mood, I found myself glad they hadn't told him. I could almost understand."

Emma said, "Well, speaking of resident vets, I was at the senior citizens' center today, or Calico House, as it's now officially called. Or maybe I should say, 'Willy's mayoral headquarters,' seeing as how everybody's so excited he's running. And the place was a virtual beehive with the news about Collin Dodd. I can't believe he didn't get the loan to build his state-of-the-art animal hospital—"

Wes nearly choked on a swallow of coffee, but managed to squawk, "No kidding?"

"You didn't know?"

"No, I didn't. Boy oh boy, now maybe we can all breathe easier."

"And it's all news to me," Jennifer said, with her heart thumping up in her throat. "What happened?"

"Well, it seems the bank thinks he's a bad risk because his practice in Omaha was on the verge of bankruptcy long before he decided to move to Calico. Elmer won't lend him the money for that same reason, and maybe a lot more, so about the best Elmer could do was give him a job helping the resident vet at the dairy."

"What about Collin's father?" Wes asked. "He's supposed to be a big cattleman in Omaha. Surely he would have the money."

Emma said, "The way I understand it, the man washed his hands of Collin a long time ago."

Feeling almost euphoric, Jennifer said, "I wonder if Ben knows?"

Emma nodded. "He does now. Irene was there when the announcement was made, and she called Ben right away. Then she said she was going to go home and fix him the best meal he's had since he got that aggravating ulcer. It didn't occur to me you two didn't know, but then how could you, when you were at the circus most of the day? Hmm. Well, that means you probably haven't heard about Elmer making Collin his campaign manager, either."

Wes frowned. "I thought Ed Dunn was his campaign manager."

"He was, but he decided he couldn't handle his real estate business and the mayoral race at the same time. He has a touch of gout, and high blood pressure, and said all the excitement and extra work was going to put him in an early grave. Needless to say, it put a definite kink in Elmer's campaign. He figured he'd use this time while Willy is out of town to his advantage, and instead, he's had to scramble around, trying to find a replacement for Ed Dunn.''

Wes said, ''Well, he must have been pretty desperate if he had to choose his nephew as the replacement.''

Jennifer shook her head. ''You know, this is really amazing. Zenobia read my palm earlier today, and she said there was going to be a big upheaval in the mayoral race.''

''And I suppose this Zenobia is a fortune-teller?'' Emma scoffed.

''She used to be, a long time ago. Now she designs costumes. But she really has a special talent for reading palms and seeing into the future. Don't roll your eyes, Emma. It's true. She even told me I had a beautiful, vivacious lady in my life, who was a great influence. She was talking about you.''

Emma flushed rosy pink, and pursed her lips. ''Well, now, I suppose there are some people who can do that sort of thing and be on the up-and-up. Hmm. You say she designs costumes?''

''Yes, and you'd really like her. Did Grandfather tell you we're invited to the party Friday night after the performance?''

''He did. Of course, that means I'll have to dress up a little more than I might have otherwise, and I can't imagine having a party in the middle of a pile of sawdust, but it will surely give us the opportunity to look everybody over, and keep a watchful eye. Lordy, wouldn't it be something if we can catch the culprit before the circus moves on to Topeka?''

Wes chuckled. ''What's this 'we' business, Emma? You have a mouse in your pocket? We're going to go to the circus for a fun-filled evening, not to play supersleuths.''

Emma waved her fork in the air. ''Are you telling me you're just going to sit there and watch the animals, or stand there at the party drinking punch, and push aside all those terrible things that have happened to those poor people?'' She harrumphed. ''Well, that will be the day. You can't fool me, Wesley Gray. You intend to keep an eye open just like me.''

''Uh-huh, but I also plan to enjoy myself.''

While Jennifer listened to them discuss what they were and weren't going to do, she considered her own plans. Tomorrow, she would check on the cub, and do a little more poking around. And hopefully between now and Friday night, there wouldn't be any more incidents.

Chapter Four

Ben watched Jennifer make the final few sutures at the corner of the cocker spaniel's eye, and said to Tina, "Can you tell me why Jennifer removed the small, inverted, V-shaped sections of the outer canthus on both the upper and lower lids?"

Although Tina wouldn't normally be dressed in surgical attire because she was the circulating assistant, she had decided to don a gown and mask at the last minute, so she could observe the delicate procedure closely. She looked up at Ben, and her brown eyes twinkled above the mask. "The procedure will cause the eyelids to stretch slightly, and draw the lashes out to the desired position. Now Jennifer is taking all those tiny stitches, or tucks, to close up, and in a blink, Taffy's eyes will be as good as new."

"And what's the procedure called?"

"Entropion eyelid surgery. It's for a congenital birth defect that causes the eyelids to turn inward. The eyelashes, instead of protruding away from the eyeball and offering protection from dust and dirt and stuff, turn inward, and scrape against the eyeball, causing whole bunches of problems, and a lot of pain. See, I did my homework. My dad stayed up with me last night to help out, and even he was impressed."

Jennifer took the final suture, and winked at Ben. "Try as you might, you can't catch her off guard, Ben."

"Uh-huh, well, why did we have to wait until the pup was six months old before doing the surgery?"

Tina's brows drew together. "Gee, I don't know. . . ." And then her eyes danced again. "Only teasing. You didn't have to wait. The surgery could've been performed much earlier, but the owner hasn't been in Calico all that long, and the vet she used in North Platte was treating Taffy with salves and lotions for an ordinary eye irritation, because he or she wasn't familiar with the condition. When the owner ran out of salve, she called the clinic, but you wouldn't prescribe medicine without looking at the pup. So she brought Taffy in, you recognized the condition, and scheduled the surgery. See, I pay attention, too."

"I didn't recognize the condition," Ben said, taking off his gown and mask. "Jennifer did, so you aren't the only one who's been hitting the books. Stayed up late myself, reading all about it, and by the time I was through, I was mighty glad Jennifer was doing the surgery. Just proves you never stop learning, no matter how old you get.''

''That's what my dad says. He's a good doctor, yet new procedures and techniques keep coming along all the time that make everything he did yesterday seem obsolete. Because of it, he says you have to keep reading and studying, keep an open mind, and be ready for the changes. More important, you have to be ready to accept them.''

Jennifer snapped off her surgical gloves and mask, and stood back. ''Finished!'' she exclaimed. ''And it isn't a minute too soon. I've been holding back a sneeze for the last hour. I have the feeling I'm coming down with whatever everybody else has. Grandfather says it's allergies, because this year we seem to have an overabundance of goldenrod in the fields. Emma says it's a summer cold, but whatever it is, my head feels like a balloon. Get Taffy ready for postop, Tina, while I call the owner.''

''Will do, and then I'll scrub down the room.'' Tina had taken off her mask, and dimples creased her cheeks. ''See, I've been taught by two very good veterinarians, to never *ever* leave the surgery room in a contaminated condition, no matter how routine the surgery. Not that this was routine or anything, but you know what I mean.''

"Did we train her right, or what?" Ben chuckled, following Jennifer into her office. He waited until she made the call to Taffy's owner before he said, "Now, maybe you'd like to tell me what's up? I know you pretty well, young lady, and I can tell when something is bothering you. And whatever it is, you brought it through the door when you walked in this morning. Can't be the lion cub, because you said he's doing well. Can't be that precocious parrot, Scamp, because we've been assured Willy's next-door neighbor is going to take good care of him while Willy and his mama are in California, and it can't be the outstanding news about Collin Dodd, because that sure wouldn't put a frown on your face."

Jennifer looked up at Ben's rugged, concerned face, and gave him a wan smile. "It's a long story, Ben, and I only have a few minutes. I'm supposed to be meeting Beth Tucker in the menagerie tent at noon."

"Then give me the gist of it in one sentence."

Jennifer sighed. "Somebody is trying to ruin the circus."

"Whoa, that's pretty heavy."

"And scary," Jennifer said, going on to give Ben a brief accounting. "I spent an exhausting, pillow-punching night thinking about it, but because I haven't met everybody at the circus yet, I haven't gotten any clear impressions. You know, when you can line up all the suspects in your mind, you can start some sort of process of elimination."

"Sounds like somebody with a grudge."

"I know, but who? The circus is giving a party after the performance tomorrow night, and we're all invited. That should work to our advantage, because all the performers will be together, and we'll be able to talk to them."

Ben grinned. "You mean interrogate them, don't you? What about the sheriff? Does he know what's going on?"

"Nobody from the circus has called him, because they are strongly opposed to asking for outside help. But Grandfather is going to talk to the sheriff today, so he'll know what's going on. I'm sure he'll be at the party, too, so that will give us one more advantage.

"Now, I have to scoot. I'll be at the circus for an hour or so, and then I'm going home and wait for Willy's call. He's supposed to call around four o'clock, our time."

"Bet you can't wait to tell him all the news about Collin Dodd, huh?"

"No, I can't, and he's going to be so pleased. Oh, and when Mrs. Cox comes in to pick up Taffy, please tell her I want to see the pup in about a week to ten days. Be sure to tell her I've used resorption sutures, and to watch for any signs of redness or swelling." She looked at Ben sternly. "And if you get an unexpected emergency, call me."

"And if you need my help, you call me, you hear?"

Jennifer gave Ben a cheerful nod, and headed for the door, tossing over her shoulder, ''I will. In the meantime, be thinking of a good motive. We have to have a motive, Ben, for any of this to make sense.''

Aware that she hadn't noticed the circus parking lot the day before because she'd arrived on horseback, Jennifer was dismayed to find the area that had been cleared and set aside for visitors quite small. It was also filled with roughies who were eating lunch. Not unusual in itself, because it was lunchtime, but why were they sprawled around the parking lot instead of eating in the cook tent? It was also quite obvious nobody was going to move for her benefit, and their faces were as sullen as they'd been the day before.

With no alternative other than to run over them, or park to the right of the circus in the marshy field that bordered upper Willow Creek, Jennifer parked the Jeep Cherokee near the entrance, hoped the vehicle wouldn't be in the way, and headed for the menagerie tent. At that moment, she only had one thing on her mind. Somehow between now and tomorrow night, they were going to have to enlarge the parking lot to accommodate the many Calico residents who planned to attend the opening night performance, and all because Papa Cannon obviously didn't have a clue as to how much Calico had grown over the years.

''Jennifer!''

Jennifer turned to see Joe Cannon hurrying from one of the tents, and she knew immediately by the scowl on his face that something else had happened.

"Beth is waiting for you in the cook tent. We've had a meeting. . . ." He sighed. "There is no easy way to say this, except to say it. Things were bad, but now it looks like they are going to get a lot worse before they get better. Jammal is missing."

"Jammal? Oh, the camel!"

"That's right. He's kept in a corral out back with the ponies, but unlike the ponies, he has to be tethered to a post at night, to keep him from ambling off. Well, the rope that holds him was cut, and he's long gone."

"Oh, Joe!"

Joe gave a heartfelt sigh. "We've been looking for him since early this morning, but we don't know how long he's actually been gone. . . . Well, Jammal is a dromedary, and can easily cover a hundred miles in a day. My biggest fear is that some farmer is going to see him, panic, and run for the old Winchester rifle."

"You have to call the sheriff," Jennifer said. "He knows the area really well, and can organize a search."

"I already called him. Good thing the mayor agreed to hook us up to the phone lines. The call went through dispatch, and it took a while to reach him, but when I did, finally, and explained what had happened, he came right out. I expected him to find the whole thing amusing, or, at the other end of the scale, that he'd be upset, because one of our circus animals is roaming his countryside, but he was quite understanding and cooperative. He has a couple of deputies out looking, and he took Gideon along with him, so now all we can do it wait.''

"Did you tell him about Rosie?"

"No. I saw no reason to. Rosie is safe, after all, and—"

Jennifer broke in with, "Well, it would alert him to the fact that somebody is responsible for cutting two prized animals loose." They were nearing the cook tent, and Jennifer stopped, forcing Joe to turn around and look at her. "Tell me the truth. You didn't tell him Jammal's rope had been cut, either, did you?"

Joe shook his head. "What would be the point? Even if he had the time, and the manpower, and wanted to conduct an investigation, there is no way I would want the sheriff and his deputies swarming all over us. All that would do is create a bad aura, and goodness knows, everybody is stirred up enough. I appreciate the fact that Sheriff Cody is out looking for Jammal, but that's as far as it's going to go."

"Is the meeting you had in the cook tent the reason the roughies are out in the parking lot, eating lunch?"

"Yeah, and they're disgruntled, to say the least. It was bad enough to settle for sandwiches when they are used to getting a hot meal, but seeing the cops, well, that sure set the mood. And that's basically what I'm talking about. The mood. We're supposed to be putting on a show tomorrow night, and it won't be easy. If it were up to me, I'd cancel the performance, and let things settle down.''

''But it isn't up to you?''

''You talked to my dad, so what do you think? He's always believed the show must go on, no matter what the obstacles, and just try to convince him otherwise.''

''I gather he knows about Jammal, but did you tell him about Rosie?''

''Nope, and he doesn't know Jammal's rope was cut, either. He thinks Jammal wandered off. Only a few people know what really happened.''

''Like who?''

''Gideon and Michaela, of course, and Beth, Lute, Frank Montano, the Riggs family, and Zenobia. Lani, Patty, and Zenobia are in Zenobia's trailer at the moment, buried under a mound of costumes, trying to keep busy to keep from going crazy.''

''And I take it Frank Montano didn't see or hear anything this time, either?''

''No, he didn't. But remember, he only works the day shift and during the performances. He can't be expected to stay up all night.''

''You need another security guard, Joe, or maybe two or three.''

''I can't afford it, Jennifer. I can barely make payroll now.''

''But can you afford not to?''

"No, and that's why I called the meeting, though I didn't include everybody, only the people I know I can trust. We've set up a security team of sorts, and we'll work around the clock. Two on a shift, that sort of thing."

"What about Mike? Does he know what happened?"

"He knows, but doesn't know the rope was cut. I thought it best to keep it from him, too. He's come down with whatever it is Beth has, and feels pretty punk. He didn't even argue when I suggested he stay in bed all day, but then he's probably thinking about his job tomorrow night. He'll be in the ring for the first time, working the cages while Lute does his act, so I'm sure he doesn't want to screw that up."

"Uh-huh, well, I can sympathize. My head feels like a balloon, and my grandfather spent the night sneezing. He thinks it's all the goldenrod covering the countryside. We've had an unusually wet spring, and everything seems to be growing in leaps and bounds. It will be a record year for the crops, that's for sure. Does Beth feel better today?"

"A little, if I can believe her. As far as she's concerned, the cub takes precedence over everything. By the way, the cub is a lot better, so at least we can be thankful for that."

The heavy, tan-colored cook tent had a screened entrance, and was connected to the portable kitchen in the rear. Jennifer had been taken on a brief tour of the facility yesterday, and had been amazed to see the large metal ovens, cooking surfaces and grill, and the walk-in refrigeration unit that looked big enough to store food for an army. Jaffo Riggs, a warm, witty man who reminded her of William Conrad, had explained that everything was run off the circus generators when outside power wasn't available, and that the frozen food was kept in a refrigerated truck, which also served as an ice house. He also explained that the meals were served in two seatings, but that some of the performers preferred to do their own cooking in their trailers. Chits, or tickets, were deposited near the cook tent each morning, which enabled Jaffo to keep a log of who would or wouldn't be eating in the cook tent on that particular day.

Now, inside the tent, a variety of odors permeated the air, but Jennifer could only distinguish one: corned beef.

When her nose twitched, Joe smiled. "Jaffo has dinner cooking. Corned beef and cabbage. It's what he considers 'comfort food.' "

"He sounds like my grandfather," Jennifer said, following Joe through the maze of empty picnic-type tables to where Beth and Michaela were sitting in the corner. "He claims besides faith and prayer, there isn't anything like comfort food to soothe a troubled soul."

Jaffo poked his head out of the kitchen doorway, and said, "Hi, Jennifer. Coffee?"

"That would be nice," Jennifer said with a smile.

"Well, at least somebody can smile," Michaela said, moving over so Jennifer could sit down. "I don't mean that to sound peevish, but this has really been a rotten day."

Beth was wearing coveralls in Day-Glo yellow, and Michaela was wearing green warm-ups. Neither woman had bothered with makeup, and it was easy to see Michaela had been crying.

Michaela blew her nose and shook her head. "I'd like to say I caught Beth's bug, but it would be a bold-faced lie. Jammal is a wonderful camel, and the thought of anything happening to him—" Her voice broke off in a shimmer of tears.

Beth gave Jennifer a helpless shrug. "It really has been a crummy day. About the only good thing to report is Zeus's progress. He's nursing, and even showing a little spunk. Lute is taking the next feeding, and he's really been wonderful. We were supposed to take turns with the feedings last night, but he took three in a row so I could get some rest."

"And I'm sure you needed every wink," Jennifer said, handing Beth a bag containing the promised cans of formula. "Where is Spangle?"

Michaela replied, "She's with Lute and the cats. I swear, she's been smiling all morning. She detests Jammal, and if I didn't know better, I'd say she cut him loose."

"I know you take it black," Jaffo said, placing a cup of coffee on the table in front of Jennifer, "but you might want to add cream and some sugar. It's pretty strong. Normally, we go through two or three coffee urns during the course of the morning, but this hasn't been a normal day. If it's too strong, say so, and I'll perk some up in my little pot.''

"This is fine, Jaffo."

"Hmm. Well, if you want something to eat, holler."

Aware that even though Jaffo was smiling, it didn't reach his eyes, Jennifer waited until he had returned to the kitchen before she said, "This is really affecting everybody, isn't it?"

Joe sighed. "In a hundred different ways. I have some things to do, so if you'll excuse me . . ."

Jennifer touched his arm. "Before you go, I think you should know the parking area probably isn't going to be large enough. I know Papa probably still thinks of Calico as a little hamlet, but it's grown a lot since he left, especially over the last couple of years. We have a mall now, a new hospital across the river, and although farming and cattle are still our mainstay, new businesses are popping up everywhere. I'm simply trying to say that you're going to have a good-sized crowd for the opening, and the people might wind up having to park in the fields willy-nilly, or down near the marsh, or out on the highway."

Joe frowned. "Looks like I should've set up advance ticket sales, but I had no idea we'd have a capacity crowd."

"I don't think you'll have to turn anybody away, if that's what you're worried about, because a lot of people plan to attend on Saturday night, and the families with kids will attend the matinee on Sunday, but the parking area *is* still much too small."

"I'll get right on it. . . ."

Movement at the entrance to the tent caught Jennifer's eye, as a tall, lanky man with bright red hair walked in. "Wonderful," she muttered. "It's a reporter from *The Calico Review,* and it isn't just any reporter. It's Ken Hering, who is an egotistical troublemaker just like his arrogant boss, John Wexler, Jr., son of the newspaper's founder. You'd better make your escape now, Joe, and I'll handle him. No, not that way. Go out through the kitchen."

Hearing the urgency in Jennifer's voice, Joe didn't argue, and had disappeared into the kitchen by the time Ken Hering reached the table.

"Well, well, well," Ken Hering said. "Fancy meeting you here. Hello, Jennifer Gray. I was told I'd find the boss in the cook tent." His green eyes glimmered over Beth and Michaela, and his smile was very wide. "Don't tell me the circus has a female boss."

"You just missed the 'boss,' " Jennifer said, not bothering with introductions. "Is there a reason why you're here?"

Ken pulled up a metal folding chair, turned it around, hitched his white linen slacks, and straddled it. "I always have a reason for everything I do. John has a police scanner in the office now, so not much gets through to the sheriff's department without us knowing about it. We know the sheriff got a call earlier this morning about a missing camel, and this is just a follow-up before John gets the story ready for the morning paper.''

Jennifer snapped, ''Story? What story? Surely you have something more important to write about than a wayward camel.''

''Uh-huh, well, in case you haven't noticed, aside from the mayoral race, the circus is big news. Can't see it myself. The last circus I attended was in St. Louis, and my seat was so far up in the rafters, everybody looked like ants. But the townsfolk seem to be excited, so what can I say? John asked me to do the follow-up on the camel, and here I am.'' He pulled a small notepad out of his shirt pocket, and made a notation. ''So, where did the sheriff finally find the camel?''

Michaela spoke up, and her voice was frosted with ice. ''Jammal belongs to me, so you can talk to me.''

A smile tugged at the corner of his mouth. ''Ah-ha, Jammal. That figures. And you are?''

''Jammal's owner.''

''Does Jammal's owner have a name?''

Beth said sharply, ''I don't know of any law that says we have to talk to you.''

His smile was still relaxed, and so was he. ''No, there isn't a law, but maybe you should consider talking to me. The story is going to be written, one way or the other, so why not let me get the facts straight? If nothing else, you can think of it as cheap publicity.''

Jennifer said to Michaela, ''With or without the facts, John, Jr., will manage to twist everything around. It's entirely up to you whether you want to talk to *this man* or not, but maybe it isn't such a bad idea after all. A story in the morning paper would alert the town. . . .''

The smile widened, spreading across his face. ''*This man*'s name is Ken Hering. One 'R'. So, can I gather by that little comment, the camel is still missing?''

Michaela sighed. ''Yes, he is. The sheriff, his deputies, and my husband have been out looking for him all morning.''

''Ah-huh, well, apparently the sheriff and his men haven't anything better to do. I have to ask. How do you lose a camel?''

''Camels can cover an easy hundred miles in a day, and we have no idea when he wandered off. But it had to be before five this morning, when my husband discovered he was missing.''

He scribbled in the notepad. ''Which means he could be in South Dakota by now. But I meant what I said. How do you lose a camel? Surely somebody has seen him. One hump or two?''

''One hump,'' Jennifer said. ''He's a dromedary.''

Amusement flickered in his eyes. ''And all of a sudden, you know all about camels.''

Jennifer tilted her chin, and replied, "Have you forgotten I'm a vet?"

"No, I haven't forgotten. Not much chance of that, when everybody keeps reminding me. How did the camel get loose?"

"We have no idea," Beth said quickly.

At that moment, one of the cats roared in the distance, and Ken shuddered. "So basically, if the camel was able to get out, some other animal might get out, too, like one of the cats?"

Jennifer clenched her hands into fists. "If I were you, I'd be careful about spreading rumors like that . . ."

Jaffo, who had been listening to the conversation, spouted, "I've heard enough! The ladies have been through a lot today, and they don't need no reporter pestering them."

Ken said, "Well, by the apron around your middle, and the spoon in your hand, I'd say you're the cook. Does the cook have a name?"

"Jaffo Riggs. That's with two 'Fs' and two 'Gs'."

"Okay, Jaffo Riggs. Maybe you can tell me where I can find the boss?"

"Sorry, but the boss isn't available. Not now, not this afternoon, and not tomorrow. We've got a circus to put on tomorrow night, and that comes before you."

Ken stood up. "Then I'll just have to catch up with him tomorrow night."

After the man sauntered out, Jennifer shook her head. "That's not the end of him, I'm afraid, and tomorrow night, it'll be even worse, because John, Jr., will be here, too, and he's even more arrogant, if you can believe it."

Michaela ran a hand through her tousled hair. "Well, I can handle a little bit of arrogance if it will help find Jammal. Like you said, Jennifer. A story in the morning paper can't hurt."

Jennifer nodded. "As long as John, Jr., doesn't make it sound like we've got a killer camel roaming the countryside."

Jennifer's comment finally brought a smile to Michaela's face. "Jammal might be haughty, and nasty-tempered at times, but he's hardly a killer. And if you could see how Spangle terrorizes him . . ." She bit at her lip, and turned away. "I can't imagine opening night without Jammal leading the elephants into the big top for the walkaround."

Beth sucked in her breath. "That's right! If we don't find him by then, what are we going to do?"

"Gideon will have to lead the elephants. We'll try it at rehearsal this afternoon, and pray it works."

"Let's be optimistic about this," Jaffo said. "Any minute now, Gideon is going to walk in with good news. You want some more coffee, Jennifer, or maybe a sandwich? I have some extras made up in the kitchen."

"I'll pass," Jennifer said, getting to her feet. "I'm going to check on Zeus, say hello to the ladies who are supposedly chin deep in costumes, and then do a little scouting on my own. I know the area pretty well, too, and—"

Jennifer was interrupted by a commotion outside the tent, that was loud enough to bring everybody to their feet.

Beth exclaimed, "What on earth!"

At that moment, a tall, striking woman with a head of auburn curls swept into the tent and demanded, "I have to see Joe, now!"

A bald-headed man walked in behind her, pleading, "Come on, Yolanda. Don't you think Joe has enough on his mind without listening to you complain about a few misplaced doodads?"

"Doodads? *Doodads!* You twit! The emerald earrings and ring I *always* wear on opening night are missing. That's m-i-s-s-i-n-g, not misplaced. That means our illustrious thief ripped me off, and I demand some answers!"

The man looked at the startled group, and waved his arms apologetically. "Sorry about this, but you know Yolanda. She puts her jewelry away for safe-keeping, and then forgets where she puts it."

"She'd lose her head if it wasn't attached to her shoulders!" a tiny, silver-haired woman exclaimed, hurrying into the tent. She glared at Yolanda. "Leave it to you to cause a fuss and spoil our picnic! You knew I had it all planned.''

Jennifer recognized Tawno from Zenobia's description, and Zenobia hadn't exaggerated. She was quite lovely. It was also clear to see she was very, very angry.

Beth stepped forward. ''Jennifer, this is Yolanda and Locke, our equestrian team, and the little lady is Tawno, one of our clowns. This is Jennifer Gray, the vet—''

Yolanda's blue eyes snapped fire. ''I don't need a vet. I need a cop! And I don't care what Joe says. Sometimes, you just have to do what you have to do. All this thievery has gone on long enough!''

Tawno stomped a foot. ''Well, *you* go find a cop, but leave Locke out of it! Every time you have a problem, you have to drag him into it. As if he cares!''

With that, Yolanda stormed out with Locke and Tawno right behind her.

Beth dropped into a chair. ''Oh, I hope Yolanda doesn't go to Papa with this. Jaffo, maybe you'd better try to stop her.''

''I'm on my way,'' Jaffo said, hurrying for the entrance.

After he'd gone, Beth said, ''Like I told you yesterday, Jennifer. Welcome to The Cannon Family Circus, where anything can happen, and usually does.''

Michaela said, ''I'd like to think Yolanda simply misplaced the jewelry, but in light of everything that's happened . . . Yikes, Joe is going to have a fit!''

Jennifer said, "I just thought of something that might be helpful. Would it take long to write down a list of all the circus people who have been burglarized, or think they have? I'd like to have it before I leave, if it's possible."

"I can do it," Michaela said, exchanging glances with Beth. "If I didn't know better, I'd say you're going to conduct some sort of an investigation."

Jennifer smiled. "Let's just say I'm going to do some poking around. One more thing, if the camel turns up after I leave, call me at home? And if you happen to see the sheriff, and I haven't bumped into him along the way, tell him I want to talk to him. Meanwhile, try not to worry. I have the feeling everything is going to turn out just fine."

Wishing she had the confidence she'd exuded in her words, Jennifer made her way to the menagerie tent, feeling a little overwhelmed, and saying a silent prayer.

"So, Yolanda is missing fake emerald earrings and a ring; Tawno, the clown, is missing money; Locke Leone a pair of gold cuff links; Joveta, who has the Canine Follies, money and a bead necklace; Noya, the snake lady, money; and Omar, the high-wire man, money and a gold chain." Wes put down the slip of paper, and frowned. "And you say the burglaries started at the beginning of this season?"

Jennifer had been home an hour, had taken Willy's welcome call, and now they were going over the list of names Michaela had given her, while Emma's savory stew simmered on the stove. Jennifer nodded. "And that was about two months ago."

Emma added a pinch of seasonings to the stew, and said, "So, do they have any new performers or helpers who might have joined the circus about that time?"

"Not any performers, but the workers, or roughies, come and go all the time, Emma."

"So it could be one of them."

"Yes, it certainly could, but that would mean the circus has two separate problems. All the accidents, or incidents, which have been going on for the last two seasons, and then the recent burglaries."

Wes said, "I take it the burglar has been getting the money and valuables out of the trailers?"

"Only in Yolanda's case. She was in her trailer, and stepped out for a minute, to get some ice. The jewelry was on her dressing table, and when she got back, it was gone."

"Was the trailer locked?"

"No, and several windows were open. Omar can't remember where he left the gold chain, though he thinks it might have been in the dressing tent, and Noya says she had a twenty-dollar bill in a sweater pocket, and then it was gone."

"Was she wearing the sweater?" Emma asked.

"No, it was over the back of a chair in the dressing tent."

"Is the dressing tent the same as a dressing room?"

"Yes, it is, and it's divided down the middle. One side for women, one side for men. It's also the area where they keep the costumes, though it's separate from Clown Alley. That's where the clowns dress, and practice their routines. Tawno keeps loose change in a jar on her dressing table in Clown Alley, and it's missing."

Emma pursed her lips. "Fake emeralds, beads, a twenty-dollar bill, and loose change. That sounds petty to me."

"I know, and that's exactly why some of them are saying Mike is responsible. It's something a kid might do."

Wes said, "But would a kid cause a fire in the cook tent, mess with the rigging, and deliberately cut the elephant and camel loose? Seems to me he'd have to be pretty disturbed to go that far, no matter how upset he was with his dad and grandpa."

"I know, and Mike doesn't strike me as being disturbed at all, in the normal sense of the word. By the way, Ken Hering came to the circus today, wanting information about the missing camel. Apparently John, Jr., has a scanner in the office now, and heard the call the sheriff got from dispatch."

"Lordy, John, Jr., ought to have a field day with that."

"Uh-huh, and we'll be able to read all about it in the morning paper. Though it might help in a round-about way. With the residents aware of the missing camel, we might get some sightings."

Wes looked at the list again. "So, do you think we should scratch off the folks who have been victim-ized?"

Emma waved a spoon. "Not if we're dealing with two separate problems. What about the other workers, who aren't roughies? Like that grumpy man. You know, the tent man."

"Tom Halverson. I'll admit he's grumpy, but Joe and Papa seem to trust him. And the list is long there, too. They have the other canvasmen, and the cage men, and the guys in charge of lighting and rigging. Oh, and the prop men, and maintenance men, and the people who handle the concessions, like the souvenir booth and refreshment stand. It's a little imposing when you think about it."

"About as imposing as a camel being on the loose," Wes said thoughtfully. "How far did you go on your search?"

"Not far, but I hit all those little places I thought the sheriff might overlook, like abandoned barns, creek areas, and the hill behind Cracker Martin's farm. I was so hoping to come home to good news, that the sheriff had called to say he'd found Jammal, not that he hadn't found a trace."

"Hmm, well, he sounded about as down as you, sweetheart."

"Speaking of calls," Emma said, "I take it Willy and Meg are okay?"

"Yes, but they're homesick, and miss Scamp. Willy was elated to hear the news about Collin Dodd, and especially the fact Collin is going to be Elmer's campaign manager. He can't wait to get home, so he can stir things up. Unfortunately, they are going to be detained for another week. His aunt is having a very hard time with this, and they don't want to leave her just yet."

"Did you tell him about the circus?" Wes asked.

"Yes, but I didn't tell him about all the problems they're having. He would only worry, and figure I've gotten myself into another mess."

Wes smiled. "Well, I don't know about that, but you're sure involved. We all are. I told the sheriff the whole story when he called, and he said he wasn't surprised. He said he had the feeling they weren't telling him everything right from the beginning, but that his hands are tied unless they ask for his help, or unless it ends up involving the town. Doesn't mean he can't keep his eyes and ears open, though. He said to tell you he'll be at the circus tomorrow night, he wouldn't miss it for anything, and if there are any new developments in the meantime, to let him know. And vice versa."

Emma's eyes sparkled impishly. ''You say Ben and Irene are going?''

Jennifer nodded. ''They wouldn't miss it, either.''

''Well, then, I'd say we'll have ourselves a fine group of amateur detectives, so how can we lose?''

Jennifer gave Emma a hug. ''We can't, if enthusiasm counts for anything. Do I have time to freshen up before supper?''

''You do, and then after we eat, we're going to go over that list again, and maybe make a few of our own. We've solved a lot of mysteries making lists, so why stop the momentum now?''

Jennifer winked at her grandfather, and headed for the door.

Chapter Five

The bright blue benches inside the big top were wide and sturdy, with each row elevated just enough to allow everybody in the audience a clear view of all three circus rings. Jennifer, Wes, and Emma had been given seats in the reserved section, and found themselves surrounded by close friends as well as Calico's distinguished notables, such as Mayor Attwater, members of the town council and their families, John Wexler Senior, founder of *The Calico Review*, and his son, John, Jr., whose head of blond, wavy hair shone like a beacon under the dazzling array of lights. John, Jr., was a handsome young man, and knew it. He also considered himself God's gift to journalism, and tried to prove it every day by printing his foolish drivel in the paper. And where there wasn't a story, he would create one. A good example of that was his piece in this morning's paper, with headlines in bold print: *Carousing Camel Canters Away from the Cannon Family Circus!* John, Jr., had gone on with his usual witless humor, all but suggesting a camel on the loose could destroy every living speck of vegetation between Calico, Nebraska, and the Canadian border in a blink, and what the camel didn't ingest, he would surely trample. He had stopped short of calling the animal dangerous, though he had listed its questionable attributes, such as spitting, stomping, kicking, and pure orneriness, and had slyly suggested everybody keep their doors locked, adding, *"And if something should happen to spit in your eye . . ."* Jennifer hadn't been able to read any further, and had vigorously suggested Emma use the paper to line the trash can.

Jennifer could see John, Jr., was still pleased with himself by the smug smile on his face, and the only thing that topped that was the arrogant expression on Ken Hering's face as he made his way through the crowd, snapping photos for the morning edition.

And not to be overlooked were Elmer and Collin Dodd, who were both wearing cream-colored suits and Panama hats, and with the exception of their wide, vote-getting smiles, looked like they'd just stepped out of a Bogart movie. The mayor wasn't far behind, with his tan seersucker suit and black string tie, but unlike the Dodd men, he wasn't smiling, and his plump face looked pale and drawn. Jennifer hadn't heard he'd been ill, so assumed he simply didn't like circuses, and was only going through the motions because it was expected of him.

Thankful they were sitting two rows up from Elmer, Collin, and the mayor, and far enough away from John, Jr., so she wouldn't be tempted to tell him what she thought of him, Jennifer looked around as everyone settled into their seats, and breathed in deeply of the wonderful smells of tanbark, roasted peanuts, and popcorn. In the background, calliope music filled the air, setting the mood, but also acting as a signal to the performers. In exactly fifteen minutes from the time the calliope began, Joe would enter the ring with a fanfare, and introduce the walkaround. Jaffo had explained it all to her that first day, telling her about the various notes, beats, and tempos spread throughout the prerecorded music that the performers used as cues. By implementing a state-of-the-art mixer, he could even make adjustments at the last minute, to accommodate acts that might be a little slow, ahead of schedule, or had gotten sidetracked by any number of unexpected difficulties that could plague a circus at the last minute. Jennifer had found it fascinating then, but magical now, as additional lights were turned on overhead, sending a myriad of colors shimmering over the audience.

Emma and her grandfather were sitting on Jennifer's right, and Wes looked very handsome in crisp dark-blue slacks and a white, fisherman-knit sweater. Emma was wearing a yellow flowered dress, and her beautiful face was alive with excitement. Ben and his wife, Irene, were on her left, with the sheriff and Nettie Balkin in front of them. Both plump with gray hair, Nettie and the sheriff looked enough alike to be sister and brother. Nettie, who was a widow, had been the sheriff's secretary, clerk, and dispatcher for as long as he had been sheriff, and she, too, was sitting on the edge of her seat, in eager anticipation. Ida, the sheriff's wife, had decided to stay home, but then she wasn't much for social events, and seemed to be allergic to everything. And with half the audience sneezing and coughing, it was probably just as well.

The floor seats in front of Nettie and the sheriff were empty, but marked RESERVED, and Jennifer couldn't imagine who they were being held for, when everybody who was anybody was already seated. And then she remembered Joe telling her that they always left a few empty seats in the reserved section for the clowns, who mingled with the crowd during their performance.

She was picturing getting sprayed with water, squiggly fake snakes, and confetti, when a voice called out, "Smile, Jennifer Gray!"

Jennifer turned just as the flash popped. Before she could protest, Ken Hering was moving off through the crowd, but not before his eyes flickered over her appreciatively.

"I don't think he's admiring just your white pants and pink blouse," Emma grumbled.

"Jerk," Ben said, scowling after the departing reporter. "I wonder how long he worked with John, Jr., in order to come up with that gobbledygook in the morning paper?"

"I have the feeling that was John, Jr.'s baby all the way," Jennifer returned, "but I refuse to let it ruin my evening."

"That's my girl," Wes said, leaning across Emma to pat her hand. "Are you sure you don't want some popcorn?"

"I'm sure, Grandfather. My stomach is in knots from all the excitement. Look! See the man in the orange satin costume standing at the performers entrance? That's Gideon Jones."

"He owns the camel, right?" Ben asked.

"That's right. He and his wife, Michaela, also own the ponies, Spangle the capuchin monkey, and Peaches the chimp, and work with the elephants."

Nettie's sigh was audible. "So many names and faces. You're going to have to tell us who is who as we go along, Jennifer. That way, we'll have names to put with the faces when we attend the party."

At that moment, a commotion erupted a few rows behind them, and Jennifer knew, even before she turned around, that the Cromwell sisters had come to the circus.

"Boy oh boy," Wes said, looking over his shoulder. "Would you just look at that."

Emma let out a healthy harrumph. "Now, if that isn't the ticket!"

Frances and Fanny Cromwell, known as "the crazy Cromwell sisters," were tall, raw-boned women in their sixties, with heads of wild gray hair, eyebrows to match, and leathery skin. Both were wearing their perennial uniforms, which consisted of granny glasses, long, dark, lace-trimmed dresses, and black leather boots. But tonight, there was one extraordinary addition. Large straw hats, topped with flowers and fruit, were perched on their heads. Jennifer was sure they also reeked of the moonshine they'd been making for years, because everybody within a few feet of them was twitching their nose. Yet they were considered harmless enough, unless Fanny happened to get her hands on Frances's shotgun, even though there were a few Calico residents who thought they should be locked up. Fortunately, the sheriff didn't agree, and tried to look the other way. They didn't sell their hootch, and used the shotgun only as a form of protection, so what would be the point of tossing the moonshining sisters in jail? Emma had gone to school with Frances, and considered both sisters nuttier than the formidable fruitcakes Fanny made during the Christmas season, but had to admit the ladies had hearts as big as the moon. After losing their farm to back taxes a few years ago, they'd moved into a secluded little cottage out on Marshton Road, where they lived frugally, but happily.

"Don't see one reason why you can't move over and make room," Fanny was saying to J. C. Fowler, the mortician. "That wife of yours is itty-bitty, don't make a shadow if she turns sideways, so there's plenty of room!"

The sheriff groaned before he called out, "This section is reserved, ladies, so . . ."

Frances was about to respond to the sheriff when she spied Jennifer and Wes, and her face lit up with a smile. "My oh my, sister, will you just look at that! It's the pastor and his pretty young granddaughter."

Fanny adjusted the glasses on the bridge of her nose, and snorted, "I only see Emma Morrison, sister. Couldn't miss that head of brown, wiry hair, Not even on a dark, winter night." She leaned forward, squinted, and smiled. "Now I see 'em. And I see a couple of empty seats in front of 'em, too. Right there in front of the sheriff. That *is* you, isn't it, Sheriff Cody? Well, will you look at that, sister. Seats right on the ground floor. Won't have to squint to see all the fancy performers. Let us through, everybody!" People moved to let the sisters through, and Jennifer knew there was no point in trying to stop them. The sheriff knew it too. He finally gave a resigned shrug, and offered them a hand.

Frances was carrying a pocketbook the size of a satchel, and managed to hit everybody on the head at least once, and Jennifer could well imagine what was inside. Bottles of hootch.

"Lordy," Emma muttered, rolling her eyes. "I have the feeling this is going to be a night to remember!"

The sisters had no sooner gotten seated, when the lights dimmed. A fanfare followed, and a spotlight picked up Joe as he ran to the center ring. He looked marvelous in slim black pants, top hat, and a long red jacket and tails, and his voice was strong as he welcomed everybody to The Cannon Family Circus, and announced the walkaround.

Suddenly, clowns seemed to be everywhere, rolling and tumbling and waving at the audience. Though the only actual clown performers were the Pie Man, Skeetch, and Gonzo, several roughies had donned clown costumes, too, to add panache to the walkaround, and add to the overall ambience as they tended to their jobs of moving props around between performances. And although it was difficult to tell one from the other with all the heavy makeup and baggy clothes, Jennifer knew Papa and Tawno weren't among them.

And then, after one more fanfare, lively music filled the air, and the large canvas flap at the end of the big top opened up. Amid deafening applause, the walkaround began.

Enthralled, Jennifer watched the procession while trying to give everybody a running narration of who was who. Omar, the tall, dark, somber-looking man who did the high-wire act was first, wearing a tight-fitting black costume bright with sequins. He bowed to the audience, and carried himself like royalty, but didn't smile. Farrah and Fordel were next, wearing pink satin and spangles. Jennifer tried to explain that the handsome blond couple were the husband-and-wife team who did both the rope act and the magic act, but gasps of delight had erupted around her. Yolanda and Locke had entered the big top astride two magnificent gray Arabian horses. Their glittery costumes were in a dark emerald green, as were the feathers in their Stetson hats, and the headdresses and saddles on the horses. As the horses pranced, bowed, and sidestepped, Yolanda and Locke smiled and waved to the audience like they didn't have a care in the world. But Jennifer couldn't help but remember that Yolanda's emerald jewelry was missing, and how upset she had been the day before.

"Lordy!" Emma exclaimed. "Will you look at that! Purple and pink hair!"

Behind the horses, at least a half dozen white poodles scampered about, while their trainer, Joveta, danced and pranced. The rather plump woman had died her platinum hair pink and purple to match her flowing dress and the ribbons and bows tied in the dogs' fluffy coats.

The performing clowns were next, and then after a musical crescendo that in itself was enough to alert the audience that something spectacular was about to happen, three enormous gray elephants entered the big top, led by Gideon Jones. He was a tall, handsome man with sandy-colored hair, and his orange satin costume matched Michaela's and the plumes the elephants wore on their heads. And oh, how wonderful Michaela looked, sitting atop Boris, the first elephant in line. Rosie was next, followed by the youngster, Yogi, but it was mischievous Spangle who brought down the house. Wearing a costume made up of orange sparkles and spangles, she scampered in and around Rosie's large feet, almost as though she were daring the supersized behemoth to squash her flat. Shrieks of fear came from everyone, but were quickly replaced with uproarious laughter, as a young chimpanzee, also dressed in orange, was led into the big top by a red-nosed, big-eared clown. Peaches was squawking at the top of her lungs, making it very clear she wanted no part of the walkaround—until she spied the colorful, fruit-covered hats on the Cromwell sisters' heads. At that moment, she broke away from the clown, did a couple of barrel rolls, and headed straight for the sisters, screeching every inch of the way.

When he realized what had happened, Gideon stopped the procession. Michaela quickly slid down Rosie's trunk to the ground, but by the time she got to the sisters, Peaches had already taken the hat off Fanny's head, and was scampering through the crowd.

"Catch that ape!" somebody yelled, and mass confusion followed.

Unable to contain her laughter, Emma wiped at her eyes and spouted, "Lordy, now I've seen everything. Look!"

With the hat firmly under one arm, Peaches was climbing the ladder to the high wire, with Gideon right behind her. Meanwhile, Michaela was trying to control the excited elephants, while holding Spangle. The remaining performers, who had been about to enter the big top, retreated. Finally, Joe and several clowns came to Michaela's rescue, and helped her lead the elephants toward the exit.

But the biggest drama was being played out on the ladder. Omar, who was standing on the ground below the ladder, was shouting angry words at Gideon in some foreign language. The music had stopped, and the higher Peaches climbed, the louder the audience gasped and screamed.

Suddenly, two men and a woman wearing bright-red satin ran out into the center ring, and within moments, one of the men was climbing the ladder. "They have to be the Flying Franzenies," Jennifer said, watching the man continue on beyond the high wire, to where the ropes, cables, and trapeze equipment hung suspended far overhead.

Below, clowns and roughies were quickly securing the net, and Fanny Cromwell had gotten to her feet, screaming, "You're frightening that poor little monkey, you stupid buffoons!"

Somebody behind them yelled, "It isn't a monkey, lady, it's an ape!" and Frances whirled, ready to challenge the dissenter.

Wes chuckled. "Boy oh boy, it's a good thing she isn't carrying her shotgun!"

Joe returned to the center ring, and walked up to the microphone. "Ladies and gentlemen, if I can have your attention. Please keep calm, and try to refrain from screaming. Peaches, the chimpanzee, is a new addition to the circus, and obviously needs a little more training. We've put up the net, in the event somebody falls, so I can assure you this little matter will be resolved quickly, and without further incident.

"Unfortunately, the remaining acts, the Flying Franzenies, Joveta and her pythons, and Lute Saddler and the big cats, won't be participating in the walkaround. But you will see these fantastic acts, and a few more surprises, during the course of the evening."

Ken Hering hooted from the sidelines. "A few *more* surprises? Spare me!"

Silence fell over the audience then, as all eyes gazed upward. The man in red had caught up with Gideon, and both were trying to coax Peaches down from where she was perched on a girder near a large, mirrored ball, clearly out of reach. The spotlight was on them, bringing it all quite close, and also showing Jennifer that Gideon Jones was a very patient and understanding man.

The minutes ticked on. Gideon and the man could go no further, and Peaches not only chose to ignore them, she scooted back a few feet.

And then somebody screamed, "Look!"

Jennifer looked up, and gasped. Tawno, wearing a bright-blue jumpsuit, had made her way up the rigging on the far side of the tent, and was walking along a narrow girder toward the chimp. She looked so tiny, but seemed very sure of herself, and paused only for a moment when she was caught in the spotlight. All eyes were on her, as she extended a hand to the chimp. For a moment, it looked as though the chimp might back up again, but then she was in Tawno's arms. No one dared applaud, or even breathe, as Tawno, carrying the chimp, continued on across the girder until she reached Gideon. Gideon took the chimp, and began the downward descent. The hush persisted until everybody had safely reached the ground. And then the applause was thunderous.

Not knowing what to make of any of it, Jennifer watched Tawno say something to Omar before leaving the arena, and caught the look of triumph on her face.

"Who was that?" Emma asked.

"Tawno," Jennifer returned. "And don't ask me to explain, because I haven't a clue!"

With an embarrassed flush to his cheeks, Gideon returned the hat to Fanny Cromwell, the music played, and that should have been the end of it, and probably would have been, if Peaches hadn't grasped Fanny's hand and refused to let go.

Gideon shook his head. "Come on, Peaches, I think we've all had enough of your shenanigans!"

Fanny was cooing and making a fuss over Peaches, and even Frances had a smile on her weathered face. "You go on now," Fanny said to the chimp. "You be a good girl, and mind this nice young man, and we'll see you after the show."

Peaches cocked her head, and let go, just like she understood every word Fanny said.

There was a short intermission then, while the performers, and the audience, pulled themselves together, and it was during this respite that Jennifer realized she hadn't seen Papa Cannon during the commotion. She was going to mention it to Wes, but there wasn't time. Joe had entered the center ring again, and announced that the circus was about to begin, beginning with Omar and the high wire act. But instead of Papa, who was supposed to be in ring three, both outer rings held a troupe of clowns, preening, tumbling, falling, and working the audience as only professional clowns could do, while high in the center ring, Omar carefully made his way across the wire, executing some pretty fancy footwork to the resonant sounds of a Sousa march.

Before they could catch their breaths, Farrah was climbing the rope in ring one, while Fordel held it taut from below. Yolanda and Locke were in the center

ring with four gray Arabians, and Joveta, in her outrageous purple-and-pink costume, was putting the
poodles through their paces in ring three.

After nearly ten minutes of Farrah's heart-stopping
performance on the rings, the Arabians dancing to a
Strauss waltz, and the poodles jumping through hoops,
tall, exotic Noya and her slithering pythons came next,
along with the aerial acrobatics of the Flying Franzenies, and more clowns. By the time the elephants entered the big top, Emma was complaining of a
headache, there still hadn't been any sign of Papa, and
it was clear the performers weren't following the roster. They had skipped over the magic act completely,
and the elephants were supposed to perform before the
Flying Franzenies. But no one in the audience knew
it, of course, and each new act brought on additional
cheers and enthusiastic applause.

But this time, Peaches wasn't in the elephant act.
Just Spangle, who not only knew how to play the audience, but seemed to know every move Rosie was
going to make before she made it, bringing the audience to their feet. At one point, when Spangle climbed
up the elephant's trunk and sat on her head, Fanny
Cromwell nearly swooned, and Jennifer found herself
gasping when Rosie sat down barely inches from the
scampering monkey.

Feeling a bit breathless by the time Gideon yelled,
"Tails!" and the elephants exited the large tent, trunks
to tails, Jennifer welcomed the break while a group of

cage men erected the complex of cages in the center ring. A few minutes after that, Joe entered the ring again. He waited for the din to die down, and then announced, "If I can have your attention in the center ring, ladies and gentlemen. May I present the amazing Lute Saddler, and the king of all beasts, Simba!"

Anxious to see the big cats and Lute's extraordinary talent, but also aware that the cats were supposed to be the last act, which meant Papa wouldn't be performing, Jennifer watched Lute enter the arena, walk into the cage, and take a stance as proud as the lion who had bounded out of the chute behind him. Mike, wearing khaki-colored coveralls, was in the cage, too, standing near the chute, and the look of pride on his face was wonderful.

Bare-chested, but for a jungle green vest, Lute wore tan, tight-fitting pants, tan knee boots, and carried a whip in his hand.

Emma sucked in her breath. "Lordy, don't tell me he's going to whip the cats!"

Jennifer smiled. "The whip is only for effect, Emma. He'll crack the air with the whip. You wait, you won't believe your eyes."

With music Jennifer recognized from the movie *Hatari* pealing over the quad sound system, Lute cracked the whip, and put Simba through his paces, which included everything from snarling and growling and trying to catch the whip with his front paws, to jumping up on a pyramid of colorful boxes. There were numerous hoop jumps, and loud calls in German that nobody understood except Lute, Mike, and Simba, and the applause was deafening.

And then, with a thunderous drumroll, Mike stepped forward and lit one of the rings on fire. Oohs and aahs from the audience followed, and then a hushed silence as Lute called, "Hi-yuh!" and Simba gracefully jumped through the hoop. The applause was instant and well deserved, but it wasn't until Simba returned to the chute and Lute took a bow that Jennifer realized the other cats weren't going to be included in the performance.

Wes realized it, too, and said, "Boy oh boy, let's hope nothing has happened to the other cats. Do you get the feeling everything is just a little off kilter?"

Jennifer replied, "I've had that feeling all evening, Grandfather, and it's unnerving, to say the least."

Emma rubbed her forehead with her fingers, and muttered, "I think I'm getting too old for all this excitement. Does anybody have an aspirin?"

"I might," Nettie said, looking in her purse. "No, I guess I don't."

Wes said, "Well, the show is over, so if we can find Beth, she's bound to have an aspirin. As I understand it, she has just about every kind of medicine a body could want in her trailer."

But the show wasn't over. Joe took center ring again, but instead of thanking the audience and giving a final adieu, he said, "Ladies and gentlemen. If I may have your attention in the center ring. Presenting Papa Cannon, and Sassy Dancer!''

A drumroll followed, and then there he was, Papa Cannon with his face painted white, wearing his ridiculous red wig, a red-white-and-blue oversized costume, and big floppy shoes. Ahead of him, circling around the center ring, Sassy Dancer, a truly magnificent white Andalusian, pranced and sidestepped, tossing her head and flipping her tail. Jennifer knew by what Joe had told her that a good part of the act consisted of Papa trying to catch up with Sassy Dancer and falling down in the process. When he finally did catch up with her, he would climb on her back and seriously put her through her paces. But not in her wildest dreams could Jennifer have imagined how rigorous the act was. Every time Papa went down, she found herself holding her breath, and praying he would get up. The act was an instant success, of course, and the more Papa went down, the more the crowd cheered.

Finally, when Papa was ready to swing up on the mount, he slipped and went down, and this time, he didn't get up. Sensing Papa was really in distress, Sassy Dancer quickly turned, and trotted to his side. Joe was in the ring immediately, followed by performers and helpers, and through the instant hush that had fallen over the crowd, Jennifer could hear her heart pounding up in her ears. Wes had an arm around

Emma, the Cromwell sisters were huddled together, and even John, Jr.'s, face was dark with concern.

Finally, Papa sat up. But before the audience could applaud, Joe stepped up to the microphone. "This doesn't look to be too serious," he said, slightly out of breath, "but do we have a doctor in the house?"

"I'm a doctor," a voice called out.

Jennifer turned to see Tina's father making his way down to the ring, and said a prayer of thanks.

Wanting to be by Papa Cannon's side, but not wanting to add to the confusion, Jennifer and Wes stayed in their seats while Jim Allen examined Papa. Finally, after what seemed like an eternity, Papa stood up, and was met with loud cheers. He waved to the crowd, and left the arena on his own, but with a noticeable limp.

"Just a twisted ankle," Jim Allen said, returning to the stands. "He'll be hobbling around for a few days, but it isn't serious."

Joe was on the microphone again, making the same announcement, and then, "I want to thank you all for coming tonight, ladies and gentlemen. The performance will go on as scheduled tomorrow night, and don't forget to bring the kids a little early before the Sunday matinee, so they can enjoy the pony rides out front."

Somebody yelled from the audience, "Did you find the camel?"

Joe returned, "No, we haven't found Jammal, but thank you for your concern."

The lights dimmed then, and Joe left the ring.

"Now what?" Ben asked.

"Everybody in the reserved section is supposed to stay seated until the arena empties, and then we'll have the party, I guess," Jennifer said.

Frances and Fanny Cromwell turned around, and their eyes were bright. "Did somebody say somethin' about a party?" Fanny asked.

Emma muttered, "They forced their way into the reserved seats, and now they're going to force their way into the party. Lordy!"

Wes chuckled. "Can't see much harm in that, Emma. Though we might have to keep an eye on Frances. If that satchel she's carrying is full of what I think it is, she's going to head straight for the punch bowl."

Chapter Six

The transformation had been quick, and quite re-markable. Lights were turned up, performers, still in their costumes, spilled out into the large red-and-white tent, and picnic tables, borrowed from the cook tent, were set up in the center ring. The food came next, and although it wasn't an elaborate spread, just des-serts, coffee, and punch, the mood was festive, as the guests mingled with the performers. It was as though a bit of the magic they'd seen earlier was a part of them now, because they were close enough to smell the greasepaint, and touch the sparkles and spangles. It was a world of illusions, but enchanting.

Along with the performers, Lani, Jaffo, and Patty Riggs had joined the party, and of course Zenobia was there to add her touch of sorcery and drama. She looked marvelous in a long, flowing Gypsy dress, and even Emma was impressed, especially when Zenobia took Emma's hand, looked down at her with flashing dark eyes, and said, "You must be that beautiful lady I've seen in Jennifer's life. Your lifeline is very long, Emma Morrison, and I feel much excitement and romance all around you!"

Frances and Fanny overheard the prediction, and Frances immediately spouted, "Romance? Why, I remember when all sorts of young men were courting Emma, and she was so fickle, she couldn't make up her mind. Will it be this one or that one?"

Fanny frowned. "And I remember when Emma said she'd rather rope a cow than get married."

Frances clucked her tongue. "That was a steer, not a cow, sister. Speaking of steers, they eat hay and oats. Now, what do you suppose they feed all the circus animals?"

"Hay and oats," Lute said, joining the group. "Except for Spangle, the monkey, and Peaches, the chimp. They like fruit."

Frances looked around. "Where is that little critter, and Peaches? My oh my, what a treat she was! Bet that old camel would've been a treat, too. Is it true they spit?"

Lute smiled. "We're keeping all the animals away from the party for obvious reasons, and yes, camels spit. But Jammal is usually a good boy, unless he doesn't like you. Are you ladies having a good time?"

"We're havin' a wonderful time," Fanny said. "Maybe we should let this lady tell our fortune, sister, so we'll know what to expect in the future."

Zenobia gave a graceful bow. "It would be my pleasure."

After the three women moved off, Lute threw his head back and laughed. "I don't know where those two came from, but they are really something."

Jennifer gave Lute a brief explanation, leaving out the part about the moonshine, introduced him to Emma and Wes, and then lowered her voice. "I haven't seen Joe. I assume he's with Papa, but . . . Well, is Papa really going to be okay?"

"He's going to be fine," Lute replied, "though Joe was right. He didn't want Papa to do his act tonight, because Papa has been feeling punk all day, and that was probably one of the reasons his timing was off. I have the feeling he's come down with the same bug Beth and Mike had. Sneezing, coughing, that sort of thing."

"Allergies," Wes said. "You've set the circus up in a field full of goldenrod. That's bad enough, but it's in the air, too, all around Calico. Won't get rid of the pollen until the next good rain."

Emma looked up at the high, pitched ceiling. "Well, let's hope the rain holds out until these fine people are on their way to Topeka."

Lute returned, "If you're wondering if the big top leaks, it doesn't. And the other tents are waterproof, too. Over the years, we've had to put on many a show in the rain.''

Emma harrumphed. ''Well, what about all the animals?''

''The animals enjoy the rain. Especially the elephants.''

''How is Zeus?'' Jennifer asked.

''He's doing really well. Beth is with him now, and I'll take the next feeding.''

''Is he still nursing?''

''He is, so we were wondering if we should decrease the CCs.''

''You might be able to dispense with the tube feeding altogether. I'll take a look at him before I leave.''

''Is there any chance we can get a look at the cubs before we leave?'' Emma asked.

Lute smiled. ''You bet there is. I'll take you on a personal tour of the menagerie tent a little later.'' The smile faded slightly. ''I guess you noticed things were a bit mixed up tonight, not to mention the chaos with the chimp.''

''We noticed,'' Jennifer said, looking around to make sure Tawno wasn't within earshot. ''Tawno put on quite a performance. I'm surprised Joe doesn't have her working the high wire.''

''He probably would if she didn't have a heart condition. It's because of her small size. Something about her heart being underdeveloped. When she signed on with us as a clown, she told Joe and Papa her lifelong

dream was to work the high wire. Said none of the
other circuses she'd worked for would give her a
chance, and all but begged them to let her work with
Omar. They couldn't do it, of course, because it was
too risky. She has fainting spells, and if she happened
to be up on the high wire when she had one . . ." He
shuddered slightly. "And then there was Omar to consider. He has a good act, and he's been with the circus
for a long time. It was a matter of priority, and making
him happy, and there was no way he would've agreed
to that kind of competition. And as far as Tawno
working with him, no way. He works alone. Always
has, always will. What Tawno did tonight was pretty
brave, but stupid. I have the feeling Joe is going to
give her a good chewing out."

Wes said. "We couldn't help but notice you took
the other cats out of the lineup. Not that Simba didn't
put on one grand show."

Lute sighed. "Fang and Ember got into a hassle
earlier today during dress rehearsal. Had to separate
them with a pressure hose. They don't have Simba's
docile temperament, and they can be a bit of a handful.
Unfortunately, we had an audience, and right away
everybody said it was a bad omen, and suggested I
take them out of the lineup. Normally, I don't listen
to that sort of thing, but with everything else that's
happened . . . Well, I finally decided to put on a good
show with Simba, and leave the quarrelsome twosome
for another day."

Wes nodded. "I can understand that. Hyde showed us a roster day before yesterday, and said, barring any calamities, that was the way the show was going to go on. He was supposed to be in the first lineup, in ring three, and weren't the elephants supposed to go on before the Flying Franzenies?"

"They were, but not more than a half hour before curtain call, Locke laid into Arturo Franzenie when he caught him flirting with Tawno."

Emma said, "Locke is the man with the horses, who's romantically involved with Tawno?"

Lute gave Emma a crooked grin. "I can see Jennifer has brought you up-to-date on the saga of The Cannon Family Circus. Yes, and Locke is the jealous type."

Wes looked around, and nodded toward Tawno, who was standing with a clown near the punch bowl. "Tawno was supposedly one of the victims in the burglaries, right? You think she'd mind if I asked her a few questions?"

Lute shrugged. "It's hard to tell how she'll react, if she's still upset. She might be tiny, and have some medical problems, but she has the temper of a six-hundred-pound sumo wrestler with a stomachache. After Locke and Arturo had their row, which almost came to blows, Yolanda jumped all over Tawno, accusing Tawno of deliberately flirting with Arturo to make Locke jealous. Yolanda's big concern was their act. At his best, Locke is temperamental, and when he's upset, the act can go right down the tubes. After that, things went from bad to worse. The two women ended up in a heap, and had to be forcibly separated. That's when Tawno refused to go on. If that wasn't bad enough, Farrah and Fordel found some of their props missing for the magic act, and somehow, the cream pies the Pie Man uses in his act had gotten dumped on the ground. So he didn't go on, either. We had to make some last-minute changes in the lineup, and to tell you the truth, you were lucky to get as much of the show as you did, and . . ." His voice trailed off as Mike walked up, and the frown turned into a smile, for Mike's benefit. "Well, now, have you all met Mike Cannon?"

After Mike was introduced to Wes and Emma, Mike gave Jennifer a wide grin. "Did you see me in the cage, Miss Gray?"

"I sure did, Mike. You did a good job."

"Uh-huh, well, tomorrow night, we'll be working with all the cats, so it should be a lot more fun."

Wes had just said, "I understand you want to be a lion trainer, Mike," when Joe entered the tent.

Jennifer quickly excused herself, and hurried toward Joe, wanting to talk to him before he was surrounded by well-wishers and admirers.

Joe had changed into jeans, boots, and a plaid shirt, and gave Jennifer a wan smile. "If you'll recall, I wanted to cancel the performance tonight. Well, if it had been up to me, I would've canceled the party, too."

"I can understand that, Joe. How's your father?"

"He says he's okay, but with Papa, you never know. I look back on everything that happened tonight, and it seems like a nightmare."

"To you, maybe, but believe me, nobody noticed a thing. They saw it as pure magic, and it truly was."

"Are you telling me I shouldn't go out there and apologize?"

"That's exactly what I'm telling you. And don't be too hard on Tawno. What she did was really something, and added a lot to the drama."

"So, who told you about Tawno?"

"Lute. But only because we asked. Do you think Papa would mind if I paid him a visit?"

This time, Joe's smile reached his eyes. "I think he'd love it, Jennifer. Might even put a smile on his face. We've just had a little to-do regarding the party. He wanted to come; I said no. This time, I won."

"Tell my grandfather where I am, and that I won't be long?"

Joe nodded, and headed for the crowd.

Although Papa's motor home was similar to Joe's, it was filled with mementos from his circus days. Figurines of performers were tucked in every nook and cranny, and the dark-paneled walls were lined with photos and posters.

Papa greeted Jennifer with a hug and a smile, but was careful not to smear her with greasepaint. Half his makeup had been removed with cold cream, leaving the other side a humorous caricature.

"Caught me," he said, motioning toward the little lighted makeup stand in the corner. "I don't bother with the setup they've got in Clown Alley. I like to take my time, putting it on and taking it off, and can't stand all the squabbling. You want some coffee, help yourself. It's a fresh pot, and a lot better than the stuff they're serving at the party." He sighed. "Wanted to go to the party, but Joe gave me such a fit, I decided it wasn't worth it."

Jennifer walked into Papa's tidy kitchen, and poured coffee into a mug. "Do you do all your own cleaning?" she asked, returning to the living room.

"Yeah, I do. Beth and Zenobia keep trying to butt in, but I'd rather do it myself. Sorry about that muddle tonight, Jennifer. Things have been far from normal around here, so I guess I should've expected it to spill over into the big top. And that includes my act. You and your grandpa were the main reason I wanted to do my act. So what happens? I fall flat, twist my ankle, and make myself look like a fool."

"You hardly looked like a fool, Papa. That's one tough act, even for a younger man. I can see why Joe wants you to retire, but I can also understand why you won't."

Papa applied cold cream to his cheek, and scrubbed. "You can, can you? Well, let me tell you, there is nothing like putting on a good performance, and listening to the applause. Nothing like the smell of greasepaint and sawdust, and even the briny odor of the elephants, on an upwind day. It's in my blood, Jennifer, and I love it, no matter how many obstacles get in the way. I know, things seem pretty bad right now, and tempers are short, but we'll get through it. Joe worries more than I do, but I guess I can understand that. He has to meet the payroll and pay the bills, and that can be a bit overwhelming when things are tight and money is short. He thinks I don't know about Rosie and Jammal, but I've got ears, and I managed to put it together. As I see it, we've got ourselves a crook right under our noses. We catch him, and most of our troubles will be over."

"Unless the culprit manages to ruin you in the meantime. But I'm not surprised you figured it out. I thought right from the beginning you knew more than you were letting on."

"Yeah, well, Joe thinks if he keeps all the bad stuff from me, I won't worry. I say he's the one who has blinders on."

Not knowing if Papa knew about Mike and the rumors, and not wanting to be the one to tell him if he didn't, Jennifer skipped over that part of it, and said, "Do you have any ideas on that subject, Papa? Any gut feelings we can go on? I know you don't want any outside help, but you can't blame us for putting our heads together."

Papa grinned. "You and Wes?"

"And a few other close friends. Well, do you?"

Papa shook his head. "Haven't got me a clue, Jennifer, and that's the honest truth. Some of the folks have been with me from the beginning, when I started out with the Folly Bros. Circus. How can I suspect any of them? And the newcomers? What would they have to gain, putting us out of business? Things are tough now, and jobs are hard to come by. They could do a lot worse."

"Zenobia told me you inherited the circus from a man named Grant Folly?"

Papa shook his head. "Is there anything she *didn't* tell you? Well, yeah, I did. It was the Folly Bros. Circus then, and I joined up as a roughie. Was in my mid-twenties, and full of a lot of resentment. I'd wanted to be an actor, as you know, but it wasn't meant to be. That's a tough life, too. Lots of doors get slammed in your face. Anyway, I knew I had to start over, and the circus seemed to be the place to do it. Grant was a good man. He paid a fair wage, and had a good head on his shoulders. He had his own troubles, though. He'd just gone through a nasty split with his younger brother, Greg. Greg took his share of the money invested in the circus, and left for parts unknown. He was long gone before I got there, but I heard all about it, and I could really sympathize. I'd never had a brother, always wanted one, and couldn't imagine getting into that kind of a hassle. See, it was Greg's fault all the way. He was high-strung, temperamental. Anyway, I worked as a roughie for a couple of years, and then started the clown act. Had me a pretty little Arabian in those days. Grant liked the act, but he also said I had a good head for business. Wasn't long before he started teaching me all about running the circus. Maybe he knew then he was going to die. But whatever the reason, I became his manager. Still kept on with my act, though. Then one day, Grant died of a heart attack. By that time, I was already married and had Joe. I was a family man, according to Grant, and maybe that's why he left me the circus. Or maybe he knew I was the right man to carry on, and make the circus everything it was supposed to be.''

''So you changed the name to The Cannon Family Circus?''

''Yep, and things were good. Maybe with a little bit of luck and some common sense, they can be good again. I've done me some thinking, see, and I've decided I'm not ready to retire my act. But what happened tonight, well, it made me face a few things. I told Joe my timing was off because I've been sneezing and feeling bad, but he knows the truth, and so do I. My timing has been off for a long time, and it's all because of my failing eyesight. So, I guess I don't have a choice. I've decided to have that surgery as soon as the season is over. Don't know if I'll be able to do all the falls after that, but I'll still be able to sit a fine horse, and put Sassy Dancer through her paces.''

Tears sprung up in Jennifer's eyes. "Oh, Papa, I'm so glad. Have you told Joe?"

"Not yet. You're the first to know. Guess you should be, seeing as how you're the one who talked me into it." He wiped his hands on a towel, and went to a chest against the wall. "Dry those tears and come over here, Jennifer, and let me show you all the old clippings. Some of them date back to before I joined the circus. Back when Grant and Greg had a good working relationship, and were acting the way brothers are supposed to act."

Jennifer kissed his cheek, and settled on the floor beside him.

"That's it," he said warmly. "There's nothing like a trip down memory lane to help brighten an old man's spirits."

Intrigued by all the old newspaper clippings and posters, Jennifer listened to Papa reminisce and point various people out, though he would occasionally ask her to read the captions. When she pulled out a clipping of two men, standing arm in arm, she suddenly had the feeling of déjà vu. "I think I know these men," she said, putting the clipping up to the light. "Or at least one of them."

"What's it say?" Papa asked.

" 'Grant and Greg Folly, owners of the Folly Bros. Circus, will be in New York over the Thanksgiving holiday, auditioning performers for a new clown act.' "

Papa shook his head. "Don't see how you could know 'em. Grant's been dead for a good thirty-five years, and Greg died about ten years ago. He was working the rodeo circuit out west when it happened. He was a big-time bronco rider, and I probably wouldn't have known about it if I hadn't read about it in the paper. Stomped to death. Showed his picture. Hmm. Well, maybe you saw the picture."

Jennifer didn't think so, but let it go, commenting instead on how handsome Papa had been as a young man. "Not that you aren't handsome now," she said, squeezing his hand. "I have to go. Do you need anything?"

He looked pleased, and a flush lit up his face. "You've given me about all the medicine I need, young lady. And you stop in again, you hear?"

Jennifer was still smiling when she returned to the party, but the warm, wonderful feeling Papa had left with her was short-lived. Yolanda and Locke were in the middle of another argument, and Yolanda had just tossed a cup of punch in Locke's face. While Locke spouted a string of obscenities, he removed his Stetson so he could wipe his face, and that was when Jennifer made the connection. The two brothers, Grant and Greg Folly, had looked a lot alike, and this man looked just like them!

Wes heard Jennifer's little gasp, and turned. "I know, sweetheart. If those two aren't something. Yolanda has been on Locke's case ever since you left, and for once, the Cromwell sisters aren't stealing the show."

"Where is Emma?" Jennifer asked, trying to keep her voice even.

"Sitting in the stands with Zenobia. Emma finally managed to get her away from the sisters, and they've really hit it off." Wes's eyes narrowed over Jennifer. "Boy oh boy, I have the feeling something is up, and it isn't the battling equestrians. Is it Hyde?"

"No . . . Papa is fine. I have to talk to Joe first, Grandfather, and then I'll tell you all about it. Have you seen him?"

"He's out in the menagerie tent, checking on the animals. You know, if I didn't know better, I'd say you've seen a ghost."

"Not a ghost," Jennifer returned. "I have the feeling it's a lot more tangible than that. Have you gone to see the cubs yet?"

"No, but Lute said we'll be heading that way soon. If we can get Emma away from Zenobia."

"Well, I'll meet you there. . . ." She bit at her lip. "Please don't say anything to anybody about this, okay?"

Wes frowned. "Can hardly do that, when I don't know what it is I'm supposed to be saying, or not saying."

Jennifer hurried to find Joe, with mixed emotions. Part of her knew if she was right, she could be on the verge of solving the mystery. But there was another

part of her that kept saying, so what? Just because
Locke Leone might be related to the Folly brothers in
some way, didn't make him the bad guy.

Jennifer found Joe feeding sugar cubes to the elephants. When he saw her, he smiled, and popped one
of the cubes in his mouth. "So, is my dad still ranting
and raving?"

Jennifer reached out and stroked Rosie's wrinkled
trunk. Welcoming Jennifer in her own way, Rosie's
trunk slid around Jennifer's arm. "No, as a matter of
fact. When I left him, he was in a pretty good mood.
Of course, that might be because we'd just gone
through all his old circus clippings, and he was probably remembering an easier, happier time." She so
wanted to tell him about Papa's decision to have the
surgery, but Papa had to be the one to tell him, though
she could well imagine how pleased Joe was going to
be. She took a deep breath. "How much do you know
about Locke Leone?"

Joe frowned. "Not much, why?"

"Don't you do a background check on the people
you hire?"

"Not usually. If they come highly recommended
from another circus, that's enough for me. She likes
you."

"Rosie? Well, I adore her, and she knows it. Animals have a wonderful, keen sense when it comes to
friends or foe. And did he come highly recommended?"

"Locke? He did, and so did Tawno. They were both working for the same circus, and were a twosome, even then."

"And when was that?"

"About two years ago."

"About the same time all the strange occurrences started happening?"

"Well, I guess. What's this all about, Jennifer?"

"I'm not sure, Joe, but when I was looking at the clippings, specifically a photo of Grant and Greg Folly, who looked enough alike to be twins, I suddenly got this crazy feeling that I'd seen them before. Papa explained both men were dead, but then . . . Well, when I went back to the party, Yolanda and Locke were fighting. Yolanda tossed a glass of punch in Locke's face, and when he took off his hat . . ." She shook head. "Maybe this is crazy, but Locke has the same face. I know he's bald, but if he had dark hair . . ."

Joe frowned. "Locke shaves his head, Jennifer. He's tried to keep it a secret, but then one day, while we were in our winter quarters, Beth saw him shaving it."

"Didn't you wonder why a man with a full head of hair would want to shave it off?"

"To tell you the truth, I didn't give it a second thought. Yul Brynner shaved his head, too, because he thought it made him look macho."

"Well, Locke is too young to be a brother," Jennifer said thoughtfully, "and I think we can count out Grant Folly, because he died a long time ago. But what if Locke is Greg's son, and he resents the fact Papa inherited the circus when, by rights, it should have gone to his father? I know I'm reaching, but what if? And it really doesn't mean anything that the man's last name is Leone. Performers change their names all the time."

"Then I'd say we'd have a pretty good motive for all the accidents or incidents. But proving it might be another matter. Even if he is related to the Folly brothers, it doesn't make him the bad guy."

"No, it doesn't, but it would give you a place to start. At least you'd have a likely suspect, which would be a lot better than having no suspect."

"What about Tawno? Do you think she's involved?"

"No, I don't. For one thing, she was one of the burglary victims, too, and she risked her life tonight, to bring the chimp down from the rigging. That doesn't sound like the kind of person who would harm the animals, or turn them loose."

They were walking toward the menagerie tents now, and Joe took a deep, ragged breath. "Did you tell my dad about this?"

"No, I didn't. I wanted to talk to you first."

"I'm glad. No point in worrying him needlessly."

"He's already worried, Joe. You admitted that yourself, and I think you'd better know, you haven't been one bit successful keeping him in the dark. He's figured it all out."

Joe hunkered his shoulders. "Even about Mike?"

"He didn't mention Mike, so I have no way of knowing. Why don't you go have a long talk with Papa, Joe? Communication in any relationship can be a pretty nice thing."

"I guess it's about time we had a long talk, huh?"

"Yes it is, and it's never too late. And while you're talking to him, tell him about Locke. I'd like to know what he thinks, and if he feels my suspicions have any merit."

They had reached the menagerie tent, could hear the laughter, and walked in just in time to hear Emma say, "Lordy, would you look at that!"

Lute had introduced Emma and Wes to Simba, and the old boy was rubbing his head against Emma's skirt. Pandora and the cubs would be next, so for now, the subject was closed. But it was far from over.

Chapter Seven

On Wednesday, Jennifer took her lunch break in the small, flower-filled patio area behind the clinic, and tried to clear her mind of everything but the mystery. It was still a mystery, because so far, Locke Leone appeared to be just who and what he claimed to be, a fine equestrian director who began his career at the age of seventeen, working as a roughie for a small carnival. The trail had been easy to follow from there, thanks to a few close contacts Joe and Papa had made along the way, who remembered Locke as a temperamental young man with a bad attitude. But they'd given him credit, too, for having the determination to turn a nothing job into an illustrious career. He had a way with horses, they said, and most of them knew it was only a matter of time before he would get his big break. He was almost thirty before the break came, and although he wasn't well liked, he was a headliner, and considered to be a prize catch for any circus, small or large.

Puzzled, wondering why, if Locke was such a catch, he had picked the struggling Cannon Family Circus over one of the "biggies" to finish out his career, Jennifer put the question to Joe and Papa on Monday, when she'd gone to see the cub. But it wasn't until Tuesday that Papa finally came up with a plausible answer. Locke was a headliner, but he wasn't a star— big difference—and sometimes being a big fish in a little pond was a lot better than having it the other way around. At that point, they'd had no alternative but to put Locke at the bottom of the suspect list, and pray for a miracle, because if Locke wasn't the culprit, who was?

Jennifer, Emma, and Wes hadn't gone back to the circus to see the two remaining performances held over the weekend, because Emma had come down with "the goldenrod bug," as everybody was calling it, and Jennifer and Wes were still sneezing. But they'd kept busy, trying to sort through the large cast of circus characters, and answering the numerous calls that had come in from Ben, Nettie, and the sheriff, every time they thought they had a brainstorm. Nothing came of it, but they agreed on one thing, at least. Two heads were supposedly better than one, so with so many creative minds working on the problem, how could they lose?

How, indeed.

Now, it was Wednesday, the camel still hadn't been found, the circus was leaving for Topeka in a matter of days, and they were no closer to solving the mystery than before. The only up side to the whole thing was the fact the cub was doing remarkably well, there hadn't been any more incidents, and Papa hadn't changed his mind about having cataract surgery. Joe had been delighted with Papa's decision, and both men had been elated when Mike announced, after talking to Wes, that he might think about going to college. They couldn't ask for more than that, and at least now, the lines of communication were finally open.

Wearily, Jennifer finished her soda and was about to get to her feet, when she saw Ben and Joe making their way toward her. And by the excited expressions on their faces, she knew something big had happened.

Ben gave her a lopsided grin, and said, "We only have one more patient scheduled for this afternoon, Jennifer, so you can give your undivided attention to what Joe has to say. And believe me, he has a lot to say. I'll make a pot of coffee, unless you'd rather have a soda, Joe."

"I'll pass on both," Joe said, dropping into the white wrought-iron chair beside Jennifer. He gave her a conspiratorial smile. "I was going to call you, but didn't want to chance anybody listening in on our conversation. I have to admit, this whole thing reminds me of some sort of spy thriller. Espionage. Cops and robbers. James Bond. Ed McBain. 'Hill Street Blues.' *The Detective,* with Frank Sinatra. And I'll tell you something else. It has me looking over my shoulder. You were right, Jennifer. Locke Leone is really Lucas Folly, Greg Folly's son. One of the guys I talked to about Locke, called me from Chicago this morning. He ran into a friend of a friend, who used to pal around with Locke, or Lucas, and remembered most of the details. I think you already know that when Greg Folly split with his brother and left the circus, he joined the rodeo circuit. Well, he eventually made a name for himself riding broncos. He got married, too, and had a son. When the marriage didn't work out, the wife left him and took their son. After the divorce, even though Greg had visitation rights, the wife and son dropped from sight, and Greg never heard from them again. Maybe he tried to find them, maybe he didn't, but the fact is, the lady eventually remarried.''

Ben said, ''And the man's last name was Leone?''

''That's right, and his middle name was Locke.''

''That's amazing,'' Jennifer said. ''So Lucas Folly became Locke Leone.''

''Uh-huh. I would imagine the lady figured that by calling the kid Locke, Greg would have a harder time if he tried to find him. This is where the story gets a little shadowy, but apparently that marriage didn't work out, either. She eventually divorced the man, and a few years later, she died of a stroke. Locke was only seventeen, and on his own.''

Ben said, ''But instead of looking for his father, he kept the name Locke Leone, and joined the circus. He must have known his father used to own a circus at one time.''

''He did. His mother told him the whole story, including the fact his father should have inherited the circus when the uncle died. The only thing is, even if Grant had left the circus to Greg, I don't think he would've wanted it, because by that time, Greg's life had taken a different direction. But I have the feeling Locke didn't see it that way, and probably felt a good deal of resentment. Which brings us up to the present. You nailed it, Jennifer, when you recognized him. Apparently Locke didn't start shaving his head until a couple of years ago, just before he signed on with us. Probably thought of it as a disguise.''

Jennifer said, ''And he would want to use some sort of a disguise, because he knew he looked a lot like his father and uncle, and was afraid Papa might recognize him. Bet he felt like dancing a jig when he found out Papa has cataracts in both eyes.''

Joe ran a weary hand through his hair. ''No doubt. So what do we do now? Like I said before, even if we could prove he's related to the Folly brothers, it doesn't make him the bad guy.''

Jennifer looked at the buttermilk clouds building on the horizon, and sighed. "Other than keeping an eye on him and catching him in the act, I truly don't know. I would suggest having the sheriff search Locke's trailer. I mean, he has to have the stuff he took stashed somewhere, but the sheriff would need probable cause to get a search warrant, and I don't think we have enough for that. And confronting him isn't the answer. If he found out he was your number-one suspect, the incidents might stop, but you wouldn't be able to catch him, either."

"You could try setting him up," Ben said thoughtfully.

When Joe raised an eyebrow, Jennifer grinned. "I think he's talking about some sort of a sting operation, Joe, and it's funny, because Emma all but suggested the same thing last night. She said I should take Tassie to the circus and get Locke to teach us a few equestrian tricks. Meanwhile, Grandfather, who has always had a 'hankering' to be a clown, can keep Tawno occupied, while I try to get Locke to slip up, or until we can come up with a way to set him up. I shined it off, because I couldn't see how it would work, but now, I'm not so sure. Maybe it's worth a try. Nobody at the circus could do it, because it would seem too obvious, but the pastor and his granddaughter? If you can't trust a pastor, who can you trust?"

Joe chuckled. "Sorry. I know it isn't a laughing matter, but just the thought of the pastor doing undercover work is a little awesome."

"Don't knock it until you've tried it," Jennifer said, giving Joe a dimpled grin. "Grandfather can be wonderfully ingenious."

"Then you think he'd go for it?"

"Does a dog have fleas? You should see what he's been doing for the last few days. He's made lists, then lists of lists, and then lists of those lists, jockeying everybody at the circus around, trying to find the answers. It's been the sole topic of conversation, and just last night, he said he thought he should go to the circus and do some snooping around. He feels the pressure, too, Joe. Papa is a good friend, and he hates the thought of you guys going off to Topeka with the mystery unsolved."

Joe gave a relieved sigh. "Then it's settled. When do you want to start?"

"We haven't a moment to spare, so it had better be tomorrow, if it's okay with Ben."

"We have a light load tomorrow," Ben said, "so you just concentrate on catching the bad guy."

Joe said, "Okay, I'll set it up. What you two do after that . . . Well, to tell you the truth, I don't want to know."

Jennifer squeezed Joe's hand. "It could be worse, Joe. Emma has always had a 'hankering' to be a trapeze artiste."

Ben let out a whoop. "Like Emma always says, 'Lordy, wouldn't that be the ticket!' Seriously, if there is anything I can do, name it, and I'm speaking for Irene, too. We'd both like to help.''

''I know, Ben, and I'll keep it in mind. Who know? Before this is over, maybe the whole town will be involved.''

Ben said, ''It already is, in a roundabout way. John, Jr., is making sure of that. After the splash in Saturday's paper about opening night, there hasn't been one morning that he hasn't written something about the 'carousing camel.' ''

''What about the sheriff?'' Joe asked. ''Are you going to tell him what you're up to?''

''Absolutely. Jim Cody is a good friend, and we've been through a lot together. If he can look the other way while the Cromwell sisters make their moonshine, he can look the other way while we play detective.''

Joe let out a sound that was a cross between a cough and a gasp. ''Moonshine?''

''One-hundred-and-eighty proof. I never saw what was in the satchel Frances was carrying the night of your party, but I'd bet my socks is was full of hootch. But they're harmless, and wonderful, even if they are slightly nuts.''

Joe grinned. ''Well, it's a good thing Jammal wasn't around. He can smell liquor a mile away. His original owner liked beer, and Jammal learned at a very young age to appreciate the frothy brew.'' Joe stood up. ''Guess I'd better be getting back. Papa has called a general meeting for later this afternoon, and I want to be there. Incidents, burglaries, and bad guys aside, Papa thinks it's time we made a few changes, and I agree. The performance on Saturday night went a lot better than the one on opening night, but it wasn't good enough, and he thinks it's time to get tough. We have too many squabbling prima donnas, for one thing, and he's all for getting rid of the dissenters, if they don't shape up.''

Jennifer said, ''That would include Yolanda and Locke?''

''Uh-huh, and that's why I want to get back and talk to Papa before the meeting. I don't think we have to worry about Yolanda. Her whole problem is Locke, and let's face it, she had the equestrian act long before he joined the circus, and she'd get along just fine without him. And that's what Papa has in mind. He figures if Locke is the culprit and we can't catch him, the next best thing would be to cut him loose. So, I have to tell him about your plans, so he'll back off for the time being.''

Jennifer smiled. ''Sounds like he's sitting in the CEO's chair again.''

''He is, and that's the way it should be. You were right, Jennifer. He's a strong man, far from retirement, and is deserving of a lot more than I've been giving him credit for. See you tomorrow?''

Jennifer nodded, but she was thinking about Papa, Joe, and Mike. Three generations of The Cannon Family Circus, working together to make it the best it could be. With odds like that, how could they lose?

It was after two o'clock when the last patient of the day left, and Jennifer could finally give her undivided attention to the unsettling feeling that she'd missed something. It had been bothering her since Joe's visit, yet she hadn't been able to put her finger on it. Something he'd said? Something Ben had said? Or was it simply her own eagerness to solve the mystery in the short time they had left, knowing if they didn't, the circus would be going off to Topeka with the culprit still in their midst? It was a scary thought, and easy to see why everybody's nerves were unsettled. And even if Joe and Papa managed to calm the dissenters, or "cut Locke loose," as Joe had put it, what if Locke wasn't the offender?

Tina had already gone home for the day, and Ben was in his office finishing up the paperwork, so Jennifer took off her light-blue smock, tossed it in the laundry hamper, and went in to say good-bye.

Ben looked up, and grinned. "I know. You can't wait to get home and tell Wes and Emma all about tomorrow. Let me know what happens, okay?"

"*If* anything happens," Jennifer said glumly. "I'm afraid there will have to be a lot more to it than simply asking Locke to teach Tassie a few tricks. We need a plan, Ben, and a good one." She sighed. "Maybe Grandfather will have some suggestions."

"Is that why you've looked so preoccupied for the last couple of hours?"

"Partly, but I've also had this nagging feeling, like I've overlooked something important."

"To do with what?"

"That's just it, I don't know. I've gone over everything in my mind at least a dozen times, but I can't seem to sort it out, and it's frustrating!"

Ben tapped the eraser end of the pencil against his desk. "Well, I've had something on my mind, too. I didn't want to say anything when Joe was here, but Irene has been concerned about the camel's welfare. I told her she didn't have to worry, because even though Jammal is used to eating hay, he's quite capable of living off natural vegetation, too. And even if he wasn't able to store water in his body for long periods of time, we have plenty of streams and the river. But that got me to thinking. Farmers have hay, and we're surrounded by farms, so wouldn't Jammal head for a farm to get his source of food? And if that's the case, why hasn't somebody seen him?"

Jennifer said, "Well, along those lines, I've been wondering why he just didn't return to the circus when he got hungry. He isn't wild, Ben. He's a domesticated animal, and maybe even a little spoiled, and I have a hard time believing he's out there somewhere, wandering around. Or that nobody has spotted him. If I didn't know better, I'd say he's holed up somewhere."

"Are you saying you think the culprit has him stashed away for safekeeping?" Ben asked.

"Maybe, if he thought the camel might find his way back to the circus."

Ben chuckled. "I was just thinking about what Joe said. You know, about Jammal's fondness for beer. If we had a brewery nearby, that's probably where we'd find him."

"And wouldn't John, Jr., have a field day with that! I'll call you tomorrow, Ben." Jennifer turned to go, and stopped, as a crazy idea flashed in her head. Suddenly, adrenaline pumped, and her heart raced. She turned, and looked at Ben. "Do you remember Joe's exact words when I told him about the Cromwell sisters and their moonshine?"

"Hmm. Something about it being a good thing Jammal wasn't around, because he could smell liquor a mile away. What does that have to do with anything, Jennifer? Whoa, you don't think . . . ?"

"He was talking about beer, but I wonder if Jammal's keen sense of smell and fondness for beer would apply to moonshine, too?" Jennifer said, dropping into the chair beside Ben's desk. "Oh, no, could it be possible? Could it be that simple? The Cromwell sisters live on Marshton Road, and that's not more than a couple of miles away from the circus. And they asked all those questions on opening night, like what does a camel eat, and if it's true they spit. There were other questions, too, over the course of the evening, and then

. . . Oh, no! Emma said that when Zenobia told Frances's fortune, she said she could see a very large riderless horse appearing in the near future, and that Fanny seemed flustered, and nearly choked on a swallow of punch. Emma thought it was odd, because it takes a lot to ruffle Fanny, but now, I wonder.''

"Sounds like you should pay the Cromwell sisters a little visit, Jennifer," Ben said, trying to hold back the laughter. "I can see the headlines now. *Carousing Camel Found at the Cromwell Sisters' Cottage, Crocked But Cheerful.*" That did it. Ben's face scrunched up, and he burst out laughing.

Trying to hold back her own laughter and trying desperately to be serious, but feeling so much excitement bubble up, she could hardly stand it, Jennifer picked up the phone and dialed her home number. She knew that no matter what they found at the Cromwell cottage, her grandfather would want to be a part of it.

It was almost four o'clock when Joe pulled the circus van onto Marshton Road. Jennifer and Wes had arrived at the circus just as Papa was about to call the meeting to order, but after pulling Joe and Papa aside, and surreptitiously telling them about Jennifer's incredible theory, Papa, who didn't think it was far-fetched at all, quickly canceled the meeting, and made the arrangements. Gideon would have to go along because he knew how to handle the wayward camel, and Joe would take them in the van. Calling the sheriff wasn't an option, because Jennifer was convinced if Jammal was at the cottage, there had to be a good reason, because the moonshining sisters were hardly criminals or, as Wes jokingly put it, they weren't "camel-nappers." And, not to be overlooked, was the new police scanner John, Jr., now had in his office at *The Calico Review*, and the *last* thing they wanted was a reporter on the scene.

Marshton Road, running between River Road and Route Five, was a remote area east of town. There were two cottages on the property, but no one lived in the cottage across the narrow dirt road separating the two, which was understandable, because who would want to live that close to the crazy Cromwell sisters, or on a secluded plot of land that was overrun with shrubbery and overgrown trees? No one but Frances and Fanny Cromwell, who made moonshine by the tubful. It was a good spot to keep their enterprise undercover, and the perfect spot to hide a missing camel.

"There's the driveway up ahead, Joe," Jennifer said, sitting on the edge of her seat. "Maybe you should cut the motor and coast in? I'd hate to frighten them, and have them make a run for it."

Wes gave her a lopsided grin. "That isn't likely, sweetheart. They drive an old rickety truck that couldn't outrun a bicycle, and I can't see them taking off on foot."

Gideon chuckled. "I don't know. From what I remember about those two ladies on opening night, I have the feeling they might be able to outrun a freight train, without the truck."

When the cottage finally came into view, Wes said, "Boy oh boy, I'd say they need to do some yard work. Can hardly see the place for the tangle of vines. Reminds me of the year Penelope Davis couldn't afford to paint her house, so let the ivy grow wild to cover it all up. Well, it covered it, okay, including the windows. I don't see the truck."

"Park out here," Jennifer said to Joe. "Even if they aren't here, they couldn't very well take Jammal with them, so maybe this will work in our favor. Get the camel first, and then ask the questions. I didn't want to say anything before, but Frances can wield a pretty mean shotgun."

Gideon groaned. "Now she tells us."

Joe pulled the van under a stand of cottonwood trees, cut the motor, and gazed at the house. "Is there a barn out back, or any outbuildings where they might be keeping Jammal?"

"I've only been here twice," Jennifer said. "Once in the fog, and once to get Fanny's recipe for fruitcake, so I haven't a clue. Do you remember seeing a barn, Grandfather?"

Wes shook his head. "I was here that night it was so foggy, and we parked around back, but I wasn't thinking about a barn at the time. I kept waiting for Frances to blow a hole through the roof of the car.''

Joe said, trying to keep his voice light, ''Come on, you guys. I'm leery enough about this.''

''Doesn't matter who's leery, or if there is or isn't a barn, for that matter,'' Gideon said, stepping from the van. ''Jammal responds to my whistle. Shall I give it a try?''

Before anybody could answer him, Gideon gave a long, low whistle, followed by two short blurts, and almost instantly, a hoarse, belching sound erupted from behind the cottage.

Gideon grinned. ''Well, I guess that answers our question. I have the gut feeling we should be wearing body armor if the ladies are around and about, but what the hey, I'll lead the way.'' His face lit up with his little rhyme. ''You guys with me?''

Creeping along the pathway single file, Jennifer found herself hoping the sisters weren't home, thus eliminating any confrontation. Wes was behind her, and she heard him whisper, ''Boy oh boy, let's hope Fanny isn't close to the shotgun.''

That brought a grunt from Joe's throat, but the procession continued, around the house and into the small clearing in the rear. Beyond that, in a tangle of underbrush and untamed elm trees that reached for the sky, the top of the dilapidated barn poked up. The grumbling, coughy, belchy sounds of the camel were much louder now, and they could hear female voices. Gideon held up a hand, signaling for them to stop.

"I think we got company, sister," Frances said. "I heard somethin'."

"You're hearin' things, sister," Fanny declared, "which just proves you're gettin' senile in your old age. Got me a good batch here, and you want to wreck it with all that caterwauling?"

Frances replied, "You want to talk about caterwauling, talk to the camel. He hasn't made that much noise since he popped up on our doorstep. Shut up, Jammie boy, or they're gonna hear you in the town square!"

Wes whispered, "Let me go in first."

Gideon whispered back, "Be my guest."

The procession started again, with Wes leading the way through the last tangle of vines. The path opened up into a smaller clearing in front of the barn, and Jennifer could understand why they hadn't seen the old green truck. It was parked under a stand of trees, and blended in quite well with the foliage. It was also full of hay.

"Well, well," Wes said, stepping into the clearing. "I see you ladies found the camel."

While the sisters gasped and sputtered, Jennifer took in the incredible sight before them. Both sisters were wearing their typical long black dresses, but had gathered up the hems with large safety pins, exposing calf-high black combat boots. They had their hair covered with plastic shower caps, were wearing yellow rubber gloves, and had flour-sack aprons tied around their waists. The old claw-legged bathtub full of moonshine was just inside the barn, and not too far away, Jammal reclined peacefully, with his legs bent at the knees, and tucked under him. He was a wonderful golden color, with a wooly textured coat, and had long, long, sweeping eyelashes. He was also gazing dreamily off in the distance.

Wes was saying, "You probably met these fine gentlemen the other night, ladies, but in case you didn't, this is Gideon Jones and Joe Cannon. Gideon works with the elephants, and Joe owns the circus."

He kept his tone light and friendly, but Frances wasn't buying it. Regaining her composure, she finally scowled and snapped, "We know who owns the circus, and we met the elephant man. He also owns those two monkeys, some ponies, and the camel, here." She lifted her chin. "We didn't steal Jammie, if that's what you're thinking. We knew he was missing. Read about it in the paper that very morning he came waltzing in, pretty as you please. Just about scared us to death to see him standing there, watching us with those big, brown eyes. Well, I can tell you, we sure didn't know what we were going to do. We thought about calling the sheriff, but we were right in the middle of our late-spring batch of elixir, so we couldn't do that. Fanny said we should lead him down the road and tell the neighbors we found him wandering, but by the time we got up the gumption to get that close to him, he'd found the elixir, and that old camel wasn't going no-where!''

Fanny adjusted her glasses on the bridge of her nose, and snorted, ''You gonna tell 'em our life story, sister? Or are you gonna offer 'em some refreshments? This is the pastor and Jennifer, not the F.B.I.'' She motioned toward some dusty lawn chairs under a tree. ''Sit a spell, Pastor. Right there where the sun is shinin' through the trees. Better enjoy the weather while we can. A storm is comin'. That's why we've been in such a rush to finish up the elixir. Sure don't want to do it in the rain.''

Gideon was talking to the camel, trying to get him on his feet, and finally shook his head. ''The old boy is blissfully schnockered.''

Frances pursed her lips. ''Schnockered? Now, what kind of a word is that, Mr. Gideon? If you mean he's peaceful and content, well, that's a fact. Our elixir is good for all sorts of ailments, including gout, ingrown toenails, warts, influenza, and that nasty old pollen that's got everybody coughing and sneezing. So we figured with that sore throat of his, it was just what he needed.''

Gideon couldn't hold back the grin. ''That's not a sore throat. That's the way camels are supposed to sound.''

''Were you planning to keep him?'' Joe asked, shaking his head like he didn't quite believe what he was seeing.

"Keep him?" Fanny replied. " 'Course, we weren't gonna keep him. Not that we wouldn't like to keep him, but we know he don't belong to us. Belongs to Mr. Gideon, here. We was gonna wait until after we had our elixir all bottled up, and then we was gonna call the sheriff. Figured he could take Jammie back to the circus."

Wes said, "Why didn't you tell us you had the camel when you were at the circus Friday night?"

"Couldn't do that," Frances said. "That was a big production day. Put up nearly two dozen bottles, and had some brewing." She lowered her voice. "Don't want nobody around when we're brewing. You'd be surprised how many folks want to get a peek inside our barn and their hands on our recipe. Used to be that way when our papa and Uncle Mitford were alive, too. Folks snooping around, all the time. We weren't going to go to the circus. Not that we didn't want to, you understand, but we didn't want to leave Jammie. But we didn't know what to feed him, either. Figured somebody at the circus could tell us."

"Where did you get the hay?" Wes asked.

"Farmer down the road. Told him we got a horse. Gave him a bottle of elixir, and he even loaded it up in our truck."

"Has Jammal eaten anything since you've had him?" Gideon asked, scratching the camel behind the ear.

Fanny nodded. "He was eatin' the plants in our garden until we got the hay."

Wes said to Jennifer, "The ladies claim their elixir is good for a lot of ailments, sweetheart, but I wonder how good it is for a camel?"

Gideon replied, "This old boy has a cast-iron stomach, so it shouldn't hurt him, but I'm going to have a problem getting him back to the circus. I brought a saddle so I could ride him back, but can't do that until the hootch—excuse me, the elixir—wears off."

Joe muttered, "From the looks of him, I'd say that won't be until tomorrow, provided he stays on the wagon."

Gideon nodded. "And I plan to see that he does. If the sisters have no objections, I'll stay right here until I can get him on his feet."

Frances exclaimed, "Mind! Well, my oh my. You hear that, sister? We're going to have company!"

Wes's eyes twinkled with merriment. "The sisters will take good care of you, Gideon."

Fanny clapped her hands. "Well now, now that all that's settled, you just sit a spell and let us get the refreshments. You pour the elixir, sister, while I slice up some nice pound cake."

When Joe started to protest, Wes stopped him. "We can't stay long, but we appreciate your hospitality." And when the sisters went off to get the refreshments, he explained. "They'll be offended if we don't accept their hospitality, Joe, and believe me, you don't want to get on their bad side.''

Joe sat down on one of the dusty chairs, and shook his head. ''I don't believe any of this. Are they for real?''

Wes chuckled. ''If you're asking me if they are genuine, they certainly are. On a more serious note, are you going to press charges?''

Joe managed a smile. ''What, and get on their bad side? No way. Gideon is going to be at their mercy here until at least tomorrow morning, so I'm all for making it as easy as possible for him.''

A few minutes later, Frances and Fanny returned with the pound cake, and jelly glasses filled with an amber-colored liquid. The last liquid refreshment the sisters had served Jennifer and Wes had been Fanny's wassail last Christmas. Jennifer remembered it being a wonderful, warm concoction of roasted apples, spices, ale, and wine, so she didn't hesitate, and took a sip. It was warm going down, and Jennifer thought for a moment it tasted a lot like the wassail, and then it hit her. The warmth spread, her eyes glazed over, her cheeks flushed, and her lips turned numb.

It had affected everybody else the same way, and Fanny let out a hoot. ''That only lasts for a minute, and then whatever ails you will be long gone. Have some pound cake. I usually add rum, but this time I put in a touch of elixir.''

Chapter Eight

Working on a third cup of coffee, Wes put a hand to his head, and groaned. "Did we just have a spaghetti dinner? Or was it my imagination?"

Jennifer held her pounding head, too, but managed a smile. "It was spaghetti with extra Parmesan, but you passed on the red wine."

"I did, did I? Well, those two ladies sure make lethal hootch. Two hundred proof, and counting."

They were sitting in the cook tent with Beth, Zenobia, and Michaela, waiting for Papa to call the delayed meeting to order, and although Joe was in attendance, he was walking around in a daze.

When they'd gotten back to the circus with the news, and explained why they'd left Gideon behind, they'd felt wonderfully relaxed, and even a little silly.

But by the time their incredible story spread throughout the circus, and they'd answered a hundred and one questions, the soft, ''moonshine'' glow had been replaced with something equivalent to a nuclear explosion. Jennifer insisted that even her teeth hurt, and poor Joe wouldn't move his head, claiming if he did, it would fall off his shoulders. Wes had taken it about the best, but Jennifer wasn't so sure now, and thought he might be having some sort of a delayed reaction.

Michaela gave an audible sigh. ''My poor Gideon. I look at you guys, and I can't help but wonder if he'll be alive in the morning.''

Beth tittered. ''And to think they've had Jammal all this time.''

Zenobia waved a hand dramatically. ''When I read Frances Cromwell's palm, I told her I saw a large, riderless horse in her future. You say they call him 'Jammie'?''

''Yes, and I have the feeling they are really going to miss him.''

''Well, we've missed him, too,'' Michaela said, ''and although they won't admit it, I think everybody else has, too. There is a longstanding joke that there are no wild camels, nor are there any tame ones, because they are supposedly stupid, obnoxious, untrustworthy, and openly vicious. But apparently nobody bothered to tell Jammal.''

Jennifer looked around the tent, and said, ''I see Locke, but I don't see Tawno. Grandfather would like to talk to her about teaching him some clown stuff.''

"She's under the weather," Beth replied. "If she has what I had, then I feel nothing but overwhelming compassion."

"You go ahead and talk to Locke, and I'll talk to Tawno tomorrow," Wes said, almost in a whisper. "For some strange reason, it hurts to say the letter T. Boy oh boy . . ."

"I think we should set it up tonight," Jennifer pressed, leaning over to give Wes a gentle hug. "But you just sit still, and let me handle it."

When Beth hitched a brow, Jennifer explained, "And while Grandfather is learning about clown stuff, I want Locke to teach my horse a few tricks."

Michaela frowned. "Yolanda would be your best bet. At least she has some patience. Locke, on the other hand, doesn't know the meaning of the word. He got into a tiff with one of the roughies this afternoon, because he was working too slow. Locke was practicing in the ring, and wanted the props changed, like now. Joe and Gideon were with you, and Papa was in his trailer, so Lute had to break it up. If he hadn't, I have the feeling Locke would've decked the poor kid."

Jennifer returned, "Well, he won't deck me, and I've always liked a good challenge."

"Hi, Miss Gray, Pastor Gray."

It was Mike, looking fresh and scrubbed, and very happy.

"Hi, Mike," Jennifer returned. "You missed all the fun."

"Uh-huh, but I heard about it. You guys sure look a lot better than my dad. He's even complaining about his teeth hurting."

That brought a smile to Wes's face, as Jennifer returned, "Well, he's not alone. He has my utmost sympathy. I'm sorry we didn't get the chance to see you work with all the cats, Mike. But we weren't feeling all that great over the weekend, and thought we'd better stay home."

"You gonna be around tomorrow?" he asked.

"As a matter of fact, we are."

"Then you can see the act. We're gonna practice with all the cats after lunch."

Jennifer squeezed his hand. "Then it's a date."

After Mike had gone to join his father, Jennifer said to Beth, "Is Tawno in her trailer?"

"Yeah, she is. It's two over from mine. Can't miss it. It's silver, with blue curtains in the windows."

"Will you be okay if I go talk to her now, Grandfather?"

"You'll miss the meeting."

"Well, as I understand it, Papa has changed the agenda, and he's only going to talk about taking down the rigging, and getting the circus ready to roll. Stuff like that. And like I said, I really think it's important to get this set up tonight. And then we'll go home."

Wes sighed. "A comfortable bed and a soft pillow sounds mighty good about now. Did Emma sound unhappy when you called her?"

"No, but then I didn't go into details, either. I just told her about the camel, and that we were eating here so we could stay for the meeting. She didn't seem to mind. She said she's been working on mayoral stuff all day at the senior citizens' center, and she was only going to heat up a few leftovers anyway."

Jennifer winked at the ladies. "Take care of him while I'm gone?"

Beth fluttered her eyelashes, and grinned. "Don't you worry. I'll take care of him, and it will be my pleasure."

Jennifer left the cook tent, and breathed in deeply of the cool evening air. The breeze was up, coming off the river, and clouds swirled overhead. The weather forecasters predicted rain by the weekend, and although she would welcome a late-spring shower, she hoped it would hold off until after they'd taken down the circus. Or at least until after Sunday, when quite a few of the circus people were coming to church. Afterward, they were having a little buffet at the house, rather like a farewell party, and all Jennifer could do was pray they had some answers by then, so everyone could truly enjoy themselves.

The shortest way to get to the "backyard" was to cut through the menagerie tents. With everyone in the cook tent for the meeting, and the roughies and other workers in their quarters, it seemed exceptionally quiet. And that was why she heard the sneeze. At first, she couldn't tell where it was coming from, and didn't think too much about it, until she realized it was coming from inside the tent where the cats were kept, and that everybody who had any reason to be with the cats, was currently in the cook tent. Frank Montano? Possibly, but why would he be inside the tent?

Scarcely breathing, Jennifer lightened her footsteps, and slipped through the canvas opening. Only one light, suspended from a tall pole, burned inside the tent, and cast an eerie glow. And then she saw the shadowy figure near the tiger's cage, holding a long prod. And she heard the angry words, ''Move, you stupid beast!''

Momentarily stunned as the dreadful scene played out in front of her, by the time she realized it was Tawno, and that Tawno had opened the tiger's cage, all she could do was sputter, ''Stop!''

Tawno whirled, and in that split-second before either of them moved, Jennifer saw the look of utter loathing on Tawno's face.

And then she was gone, her tiny body slipping through the canvas fold at the back of the tent. And Fang. Oh, no, Fang! He had slipped away, too, almost like an apparition.

With her heart nearly pounding out of her chest, Jennifer raced for the cook tent, bursting in finally and screaming, "Tawno let Fang out! I saw her, and Fang is out of his cage!"

Complete bedlam followed, but Papa quickly took charge, his voice clear and strong as he said, "You people know enough to keep calm in this kind of an emergency, so I'm not going to take the time to remind you. Arturo, go to the roughies' quarters and tell them to be on the alert. Anthony, find Frank, now! Lute and Mike, go look for the cat. Joe and Omar, you come with me. We're going to find Tawno."

White-faced and visibly shaken, Locke piped up, "Can't be Tawno. She's feeling lousy. Head all stuffed up. She wouldn't do something like that. Can't be Tawno, no way."

Papa muttered, "Quit your babbling, Locke, and stay put."

"But I can help," Locke protested.

"You were told to stay put," Joe returned, "and that's the way it's going to be until we get this sorted out."

Jennifer dropped to the bench beside her grandfather, and took deep, ragged breaths. She understood Papa and Joe's reasoning. They had no way of knowing if Tawno had acted alone, or if Locke had been a part of it with her, and they weren't going to take any chances.

Wes put an arm around Jennifer's shoulders. "You okay, sweetheart? You're trembling."

"I-it was terrible, Grandfather. She looked so angry, like she hated the world. And she had a prod. Probably the one she used to goad Rosie into running."

"Did she see you?" Beth asked.

"She did, and that's why she ran. Fang was already out of the cage by the time I got there, and there was nothing I could do."

Anger filled Michaela's eyes, as she exclaimed, "Papa! We have to check the rest of the animals. Who knows what other damage she's done!"

Papa nodded. "Skeetch and Gonzo, go with Michaela. Check the elephants, the corral, and the stable. Fordel and Elijah, check on Spangle and Peaches. Noya, you can check on your snakes, but I want the rest of you to stay right here. I'm putting the pastor in charge. Jennifer and Beth will be here if you find any injured animals, and Jaffo, call the sheriff! I might be breaking a cardinal rule, but it's my decision to make."

Papa's voice trailed off, and he quickly left the tent with Joe.

"You're mistaken," Locke said, glaring down at Jennifer. "You saw somebody else; you didn't see Tawno."

Jennifer had to bite her tongue to keep from spewing out all the things she knew about him, but if he was innocent, what would be the point? And if he wasn't, he could be dangerous. Trying to get control of her voice, she said, "You have every reason to be upset, Mr. Leone,'' and dismissed him by looking away.

But Locke wasn't about to be dismissed, and was prepared to do battle, and probably would have, if Yolanda hadn't stepped in.

''I told you that woman was trouble the first time I met her, you twit!'' she cried. ''But would you listen? Oh, no. So you've had a big thing going with her for a long time. Big deal. Just shows you how dumb some people can be.''

When Locke pulled Yolanda off to a secluded corner, Jennifer sighed. ''Tell me this isn't happening.''

''It's happening,'' Zenobia grumbled, ''and I should've foreseen it. I tell fortunes, right? And I make a big deal out of my talent, and yet I won't look into the future of the circus, because I'm afraid of what I'll see.''

Jennifer admonished, ''It's not your fault all these things are happening, Zenobia. So don't blame yourself. Let's listen to Grandfather, and try to stay calm.''

Wes had gone up to the head table, and after only a few moments, he had managed to give the confused, frightened crowd a bit of stability. He led the group in prayer and song, and even told a few corny jokes, trying to put smiles on their faces.

''He's really something,'' Beth said fondly. ''You're very lucky to have him for your grandfather.''

"Believe me, I know. And you are all very lucky to have Joe and Papa."

Zenobia muttered, "I said it before, and I'll say it again. In fact, I'll keep right on saying it until this nightmare is over. Papa and Joe are good, decent men, and don't deserve this kind of rubbish falling on their heads."

Jennifer poured coffee into her cup from the carafe on the table, and found that her hands were still shaking. "Where would Fang go?" she asked Beth finally.

"It's hard to say, but there is a lot of space out there. The fields, the farmland, the creek, and the plateaus beyond. I imagine he would want to go someplace high. I'm sure he's frightened, and when you have a frightened, unpredictable tiger—"

The words were barely out of Beth's mouth, when Omar rushed in with the news. They'd found Tawno. She was up in the rigging in the big top, threatening to jump, and they wanted Wes to try to talk her down.

At that moment, all control was lost. Everybody spilled out of the cook tent, and headed for the big top.

Not surprised to see the sheriff and two of his deputies, only that they'd gotten to the circus so soon, Jennifer heaved a sigh of relief, because the sheriff had already taken charge, treating the situation as he would with any suicidal jumper. Nets had been raised across all three rings, and the deputies were effectively keeping everybody back. But what was a surprise was the absence of reporters. When she asked Wes about it, he replied, ''Jaffo called the sheriff at home, sweetheart. Was that smart, or what? Now let's see what we can do to get that little lady safely down, and if you want to say a few prayers, it sure wouldn't hurt.''

After speaking with her grandfather, Jennifer sat in the stands with Beth and Zenobia, while the drama unfolded. The spotlights were on, illuminating the tiny figure high above their heads. Tawno was wearing the same blue jumpsuit she'd worn on opening night, but that night, she'd climbed the rigging to rescue the chimp. Jennifer couldn't comprehend how they could be one and the same person.

Papa had set up the PA system so Wes could talk to the woman without hollering, and the silence around them was almost tangible as he spoke to her in calm, soothing words.

Remembering how easily Tawno had maneuvered the girders before, Jennifer wasn't concerned about her falling, unless she fainted or deliberately jumped, but she still held her breath when Tawno backed up. And then Jennifer's breath caught in her throat. Not more than five feet behind the silver-haired lady, the spotlight had picked up the cat, crouched low and ready to spring. It was obvious Tawno didn't see it, and Jennifer could almost hear the silent screams of the onlookers, threatening to erupt from their throats.

Joe saw the cat, too, and spoke to Omar, who went running out of the big top to find Lute and Mike. And

then Joe was talking to Tawno, trying to find a way
to talk her down, without alerting her to the cat.

Later, when Jennifer thought about it, she could
only describe what happened next as something right
out of a dream. Everything seemed to be happening in
slow motion. The cat growled, Tawno turned, and over
she went, free-falling into the net. There was no holding back the screams then, and they echoed through
the air. A scattering of nervous applause followed, as
the sheriff, Papa, Joe, and Locke helped Tawno down
from the net. The sheriff spoke to one of the deputies,
who took Tawno and Locke away, but the excitement
wasn't over yet. The cat was still crouched high above
them, its orange-and-black body aglow in the spotlight.

Everybody breathed a sigh of relief when Lute and
Mike ran into the big top, but the sighs quickly
changed to cries of disbelief when they realized Mike
was going up.

Beth sucked in her breath. "Oh, no!"

Feeling a little light-headed, Jennifer asked, "Has
Mike ever been up on the rigging before?"

"Lots of times, but this is different."

"Maybe not. How does Mike get along with
Fang?"

"Probably better than Lute, but . . ."

"Then that's probably why Lute is letting him go
up."

For the next ten minutes, Jennifer watched in awe as Mike sat up on a girder not more than three feet from the cat, talking to it, maybe even pleading. But it wasn't until she saw Lute move to the far side of the tent that she realized what they were trying to do. And unbelievably, it worked. Suddenly, the cat backed up, turned around, and followed the maze of lighting platforms, trestles, and girders down, to where Lute was waiting with a collar and leash.

This time, the applause was deafening, and in a heartbeat, it was over.

Jennifer was out of the stands in an instant, and ran into Wes's waiting arms.

"Well, that's one way to forget about a hangover," he said, holding her close. "You want to go home? Or do you want to get the rest of the story?"

"I'd like to stay," Jennifer said, drinking in the comfort of his arms. "But only if you feel like it."

He gave her a wink. "I was hoping you'd say that, because I sure wouldn't want to go home and face Emma without being able to give her the ending. Boy oh boy, is this gonna be a night to remember."

It was late when Jennifer and Wes let themselves into the house, but Emma was still up, sitting in her reading chair, wearing a flowered housecoat, and trying very hard to put a smile on her face.

"The minute you called to tell me you'd be late, I knew something had happened," she said, eyeing them intently. "And I was right, from the looks of you. Well, you just sit down while I fix you some tea, and then I want to hear every detail. I built a fire because we still have a nip in the air, but . . ." She bit at her bottom lip. "Something bad has happened, hasn't it?"

While they drank tea in front of the cozy fire, Wes started from the beginning, but let Jennifer take over when he got to the unbelievable ending.

"Tawno and Locke were taken to Papa's motor home," Jennifer said, "and we were fortunate. We were able to sit in on the questioning. By that time, Locke was in pretty bad shape. He admitted who he was, but his reasons for joining The Cannon Family Circus were totally innocent. He knew all about his father and uncle, but blamed his father for the split, so he wasn't surprised when the uncle left the circus to Papa. And Papa was right. Locke was a headliner, but wasn't a star, and like Papa said, sometimes it's better to be a big fish in a little pond than the other way around. The only thing is, he was afraid to go to Papa and tell him who he was. He wasn't sure of the time frame, meaning when his father actually split with the uncle, and for all he knew, his father had been on the outs with Papa, too. So he decided to play it safe. While he was with the Sarazan Circus, he met Tawno, and told her the whole story. She thought he was crazy, and said he should march right up to Papa and demand what was rightfully his."

"So she decided to do it for him, in a roundabout way?" Emma asked.

Wes said, "Yes, but that wasn't her only reason. Her dream was to work the high wire, and she figured if Locke had the circus, he would let her be a high-wire star. She thought if she made enough trouble for the circus, Papa would be forced to sell out, and Locke would be right there to pick up the pieces."

Emma shook her head. "The woman sounds ill."

Jennifer said, "I don't think she's ill, Emma, just disturbed. But it won't stop her from being punished for what she's done to the circus. She's up against some pretty serious charges, and she won't walk away with a pat on her hand."

"And Locke?"

"He feels terrible, and thinks it's his fault. Papa and Joe disagree, of course, and want him to stay on. He'll finish out the season, but nobody knows what will happen after that. Well, that's not exactly the truth. We know Papa is going to have eye surgery, and we know the world is full of fresh starts and second chances."

Emma nodded. "Lordy, if that isn't the truth. And you say those nutty Cromwell sisters aren't in trouble for hiding the camel?"

They hadn't told Emma about the moonshine they'd consumed, and Jennifer lowered her eyes. They would eventually tell her, but not now, not tonight. "No, they aren't in trouble. What they did was purely innocent."

"You call making moonshine innocent?" Emma harrumphed. "Well, I guess I'm glad they didn't get in trouble. They've never harmed a living soul, and I know they've got big hearts, even if their brains are the size of peas. What about the money and jewelry Tawno took? Did she hand it over?"

Wes put another log on the fire, and shook his head. "Nope, and that's the strange part. She claims she didn't steal anything from anybody. Can't imagine why she would lie about something like that, when she fessed up to everything else. Not that it matters. Tomorrow is a new day, full of new beginnings."

"Amen," Emma said through a shimmer of tears. "Lordy, if that isn't the ticket. Tears when we should be smiling. Made a pound cake when I found out you weren't coming home for supper. Figured it might taste good after all that circus food."

Jennifer exchanged smiles with Wes, and said, "Pound cake sounds wonderful, Emma, and you're wonderful."

Emma flushed rosy pink, and walked into the kitchen.

Chapter Nine

It had been a wonderful day, with church services in the morning and the buffet in the afternoon, that stretched into several warm, fun-filled hours. And then there were the lingering few folks who had added a bit of poignancy to the moment, because the circus was leaving tomorrow, and nobody wanted to say good-bye.

Not everyone who was invited came, but those who had would be tucked away in that special place in the mind where memories were kept, and they would always be thought of as good friends. Like Papa, in his outrageous flowered tie, and Joe and Mike, whose love and camaraderie had brightened the day. And Beth, wearing a Day-Glo orange dress, and dramatic Zenobia, with her flowing skirt and Gypsy bangles. Lute hadn't come because he had so many things to do, but Jennifer suspected he hadn't wanted to come, because he wasn't a churchgoing man. But he'd sent along his love. Patty Riggs had stayed behind, too, because the Pie Man, Elijah Shaw, was on the shy side, and didn't mingle well with people. But Lani and Jaffo were there, arriving a little late, and loaded down with dishes to add to the buffet. But the real treat had been Spangle, dressed in a blue pinafore that matched Michaela's skirt and Gideon's tie. She'd been an angel in church, behaving better than some of the parishioners' children, and later at the house, she'd spent most of the time giving out smacking kisses, or sitting on Gideon's shoulder.

Now, while Wes finished up some paperwork at the church, Jennifer and Emma were sharing a few quiet moments on the front porch, as stars blinked off and on in the sky, and the air around them was filled with the sweet smells of late spring—rich loam, Emma's roses, and just a trace of the mint Emma had planted near the house. It was all a prelude to summer, and not even the ominous clouds on the horizon could darken the mood.

"Well, at least the rain held off," Emma said, pouring iced tea into tall glasses from the pitcher on the little side table. "Now they're saying we won't get the brunt of the storm until Tuesday or Wednesday. That's good, too. The circus folks should be well on their way to Topeka by then.'' She sighed. ''I'm going to miss them.''

''We all are,'' Jennifer said. ''The party was a huge success, Emma, and we've all been left with a lot of fond memories. . . .'' Her words trailed off as Wes joined them, and by the scowl on his face, it was easy to see he wasn't happy.

''Oh-oh,'' Emma said. ''I know that look. Either you've misplaced some important papers, or you found chewing gum in one of the pews.''

Wes sat down, and ran a hand through his white hair. ''Don't I wish it were something that simple. Dear God, help us all. I was in a hurry to get out of church today because of the party, so instead of emptying the collection plate, I left it on my desk. Well, all of the silver is gone. Dimes and quarters mostly, and although I didn't count it, I'd say there was close to ten dollars.''

Emma said, ''Lordy, what is this world coming to, when people can rob a church!''

''Didn't you put the collection plate in your office after the service?'' Jennifer asked.

''I did, but it was before the church emptied out. I put it on my desk, and then went into the vestibule to talk to everyone.''

Emma frowned. ''And left the door open, I would imagine.''

''Yes, unfortunately. And we had an exceptionally large crowd today, because everybody wanted to see the circus performers, so I'll probably never know who took it. It breaks my heart to think we have a thief in the congregation, but what else can I believe?''

''Where there any bills, Grandfather?''

''Uh-huh. I remember several ones and a couple of fives. I know, you're wondering why the culprit didn't take the currency.''

Emma pursed her lips. ''Sounds like a kid to me. A little kid, who would prefer shiny coins over wrinkled old bills, and don't forget, we had a good many little kids in attendance. Too many, if you ask me. I think we should start up the Sunday-school classes again, and give the adults a chance to enjoy the service in peace.''

''I'll consider it,'' Wes said wearily. ''But right now, I'm going to turn in. It's been a long day.''

''He's really upset,'' Jennifer said after Wes went in the house.

''I know, and I don't blame him. He's a good man with a big heart, and he'd like to think he can trust everybody. Then when something like this happens, it just makes him realize he can't. And that's what's so sad. But he'll get over it, Jennifer. And like he said the other night, tomorrow is a new day, and full of new beginnings. You want to sit a spell longer? If so, I'd better get us some sweaters.''

''I'd like to stay out here a little longer, Emma. I think I have a sweater hanging on the coat rack.''

"If not, you can use one of mine. No point climbing those stairs when a body doesn't have to. Won't be but a minute."

But when one minute stretched into five, and then ten, Jennifer became alarmed. Had something happened to Emma, or to her grandfather? She was just about to go in the house, when Emma walked out with heavy footsteps and a downcast expression on her pretty face.

Emma handed Jennifer a sweater, plopped down in the chair, and hugged her arms close to her body. "Well, it looks like the thief didn't stop with the collection plate. Somebody was in my jewelry box, Jennifer, and quite a few things are missing."

Shocked and baffled, Jennifer exclaimed, "Oh, Emma!"

"Not that I've got all that much in the way of jewelry, you understand, but some of the missing pieces are special. Like my mother's cameo brooch and the gold earrings your granddaddy gave me a couple of years ago. Can't find my little heart-shaped locket, either, or the gold sweater guard with all the pearls. I hate to say it, but it had to be somebody from the circus. There weren't any parishioners at the party, and everything was right there earlier this morning. I know that for a fact because I almost wore the earrings. Even tried them on."

Jennifer went over everybody who had come to the party, and quickly eliminated every one of them, but remembered too, that Emma's bedroom was right off the kitchen, which would have given the thief easy access. Jennifer sighed. "Those people have become our dear friends, Emma. How can we accuse any of them?"

Emma's sigh was heartfelt, too. "More importantly, what do we do about it? Tawno said she wasn't responsible for the thefts, so maybe she was telling the truth. Maybe it's somebody else."

"Somebody who was here today. You don't suppose . . ."

Emma shuddered, as though she could hardly bear the thought. "I know, it crossed my mind, too. Maybe all those people who thought Mike was the culprit, were right. Only they were looking at it as a single problem, when all along, they had two offenders. Joe and Papa will have to be told, honey, as hard as that sounds."

"But we don't have any proof. . . ."

"So, if it isn't Mike, it has to be Joe, or Papa, or Beth, or Zenobia, or Michaela, or Gideon, or Jaffo, or Lani. Which one would you choose?"

Jennifer felt the sting of hot tears behind her eyes, and shook her head. "This is so sad, I can hardly stand it, Emma. Those people are our friends. How can you sort through something like that, and come up with a plausible answer?"

"You can't, but remember, whoever it is, did it to the circus, too. It's getting late. We'd better wait until morning to tell your granddaddy, and maybe he'll know how to handle it.''

''Until tomorrow, then,'' Jennifer said, kissing Emma's cheek. But as she headed up the stairs, her heart felt heavy with grief as she remembered her grandfather's words. *''Tomorrow is a new day and full of new beginnings.''* Tomorrow was also going to be one of the most difficult days of their lives.

With the big top down and most of the colorful trucks loaded, it still wasn't easy to find a place to park, because everybody seemed to be scurrying around. Wes pulled in as close as he could to Papa's motor home, and took a deep breath. ''I don't see Papa or Joe anywhere, unless they're in the motor home. Well, we're not going to talk to anybody but them, sweetheart. Dear Lord, I hate this. I'd rather cut off my foot.''

Jennifer looked out at the long line of vehicles, knowing how much magic was tucked away inside each and every one of them, and thought back to the last few hours. They'd tried to eat breakfast as they searched for an answer, and prayed for God's guidance. They'd all spent a terrible night, too, but at least Wes had been spared a few hours before being told about Emma's missing jewelry. Not that it mattered. The pain had been just as intense, and now their hearts were as heavy as the threatening storm clouds that swirled overhead.

The elephants, the last to be loaded because they were used as beasts of burden as well as performers, were staked out under a tree. Gideon was with them, and waved, as did Zenobia, as she hurried toward her trailer.

Jennifer frowned. "Does everything look slightly off kilter here? Or is it my imagination?"

"Right about now, I think the whole world is slightly off kilter," Wes said. "But I agree with you. If you want the truth, they look like they're searching for something."

"Maybe the thief struck again," Jennifer muttered, getting out of Wes's sedan. The wind was up, and she pulled her jacket close.

Wes joined her on the passenger side of the car, and stuffed his hands in his pockets. "Shall we see if Papa is in the motor home?"

"No need to, Grandfather. Here he comes."

Papa's smile was as cheerful as his steps. "Well, you, too," he said, shaking Wes's hand and giving Jennifer a hug. "This is a surprise. I thought you said you didn't want to watch us pull away, and that's why we said our good-byes yesterday."

"Had a change of plans," Wes said, managing a smile. "Is Joe around?"

Papa rolled his eyes. "He is, and like everybody else, he's fit to be tied. We'd be ready to roll by now if that mischievous monkey hadn't turned up missing."

"Spangle?" Jennifer said.

"None other. We've been looking for her for a good hour, and Michaela is having a fit. 'Course, everybody else is having a fit, too. We wanted to be on the road before the storm hits, and we still have to load up the elephants."

Wes said, "Well, would it be possible to talk to you and Joe for a few minutes before you leave? No hurry. As a matter of fact, we can help you look for Spangle. . . ."

Papa frowned. "It sounds serious."

"Could be. But we'd better wait until—"

At that moment, somebody yelled, "I found her! Hey, you all, I found her!"

A tall, thin roughie with a head of curly blond hair was standing near one of the oversized trucks, shaking his head. Word got around, and within minutes, a crowd had gathered. Out of breath, Michaela pushed through, and said, "Oh, brother! Why didn't I think of this. She's in Rosie's truck!"

Papa chuckled. "So, the little varmint has been hiding in Rosie's truck. Tan her britches, Michaela, and give her what-for."

Joe had arrived just as Spangle let out a screech from inside the truck. And then Michaela's voice: "You little dickens. Do you know we've been looking everywhere for you? Oh, no! Papa! Joe! You'd better come look at this!"

Without a clue, Papa and Joe climbed up the ramp, and walked into the truck. Gideon joined Jennifer and Wes, and shrugged. "You've got me."

A few minutes later, Michaela appeared with Spangle in her arms, and her face was flushed. "You're not going to believe it," she kept saying, over and over again. "I'm so embarrassed!"

A few minutes later, Papa and Joe walked out of the truck, and they looked pretty sheepish, too. "Somebody better get us a box," Papa said. "We've found our thief, and the loot. Spangle has had it stashed in Rosie's truck all along."

Not knowing whether to laugh or cry, Jennifer simply hugged her grandfather, and gave thanks to God. Their prayers had been answered!

"More coffee?" Papa said, grinning at the impish monkey Jennifer held in her arms.

They were sitting in Papa's motor home with Michaela and Gideon, and Jennifer cuddled Spangle close. Spangle clung to Jennifer, like she knew she was in trouble, but that didn't stop her from giving an occasional smacking kiss.

"No more coffee for me," Wes said, picking up the earrings he'd given Emma. "You know, I never thought she liked them, but the way she carried on this morning, you'd have thought they were the crown jewels."

Michaela said, "Well, will you please give her my deepest apologies?"

Gideon chuckled. "So you had your suspect list all made up, and were about to bust us when the truth came out. But seriously, you have my apologies, too. I'd also given it some thought. Even before all this happened, I kept asking myself why I was dragging my feet about leaving. Like last night. I had a dozen things to do, and all I could think about was the look on the Cromwell sisters' faces when I rode off with Jammal. They were crushed. I really wanted to do something nice for them, because even with all the moonshine he consumed, those gals took good care of him. And now I think I have the answer. Spangle is like a little kid. A jealous little kid. We've had her a long time, and she never did anything like this before. So, after doing a little backtracking, it occurred to me that all the trouble started about the same time we got Peaches."

Papa grinned. "Are you saying she's taken to stealing because she's jealous?"

"That's exactly what I'm saying. The pecking order has been disturbed."

Michaela ran a hand over Spangle's head, and tweaked her under the chin. "And you want to give Peaches to the sisters?"

"Only if they want her," Gideon said. "If not, then we'll just have to find a home for her somewhere else. She's a sweetie, but she's almost impossible to train, so she would definitely make somebody a better pet than she'll ever make a circus performer. And I know Spangle will be a lot happier if she isn't around. What do you think, Mich?"

Michaela nodded. "I think it's a wonderful idea."

"And so do I," Jennifer said, with happiness bubbling up. "And even if the sisters don't want her, I can find her a home. But you know, I don't think it will come to that. They were quite taken with Peaches on opening night, and Peaches would certainly give them something to think about, other than making moonshine. If it's okay—it would also save you some time—we'll take Peaches with us, and stop by the cottage before we go home."

Wes grinned, and there was a twinkle in his eyes when he said, "Boy oh boy, can't you just see it? A rambunctious chimp full of moonshine?"

"No way," Jennifer said sternly. "A chimp doesn't have a camel's digestive system, and drinking alcohol could do a lot of damage. I'll have to make it clear to them. Absolutely no moonshine, or elixir, for the chimp!"

Spangle was making little chortling sounds near Jennifer's ear, and Jennifer gave her a hug. "Well, you got your way, didn't you, you little minx? And I'll bet you think you're pretty clever."

"You want my opinion, I think she's darned clever," Wes said, patting Spangle's head. "First of all, she wears those pinafores with the big pockets all the time, and what better place to carry around the loot? And then there's that necklace she wears. She could have a whole bunch of coins jangling around, and nobody would know it. Then, when you consider she hid the loot in her best friend's truck, who just happens to be a ten-ton elephant, well, you tell me if she isn't one smart monkey.''

"Maybe we should change your wearing apparel, little lady,'' Michaela said fondly. "Something without pockets.''

Papa said, "Uh-huh, well, if anything turns up missing after this, at least we'll know where to look.''

A few minutes later, Jennifer and Wes went with Gideon to get the chimp, and it was time to say good-bye. A tearful good-bye, because The Cannon Family Circus was full of some of the nicest people they'd ever known.

"You okay?'' Wes asked, as he pulled up in front of the sisters' cottage. "Peaches has been jabbering away, but you've been awfully quiet.''

Jennifer smoothed down the chimp's blue, frilly pinafore, and gave Wes a smile. "I'm okay. I was just thinking about Simba, Pandora, and the cubs, and remembering the walkaround on opening night, and all the magic I felt. It was so hard to say good-bye.''

"I know, sweetheart, but at least we were spared the terrible task of pointing a finger. We were wrong, and I thank the dear Lord we were.''

Suddenly, Peaches began to scramble around and scream with excitement. Jennifer grinned. "Here come the sisters, and you can't tell me Peaches doesn't recognize them!"

With their gray hair and long skirts blowing in the wind, Frances and Fanny's faces were alive with laughter and joy as Peaches bounced out of the car, and straight into their arms.

"My oh my," Frances exclaimed. "Will you just look at this! It's our little friend from the circus."

"She's yours if you'd like to keep her," Jennifer said, taking in the wonderful picture the threesome presented. "If you can't keep her, I'll find her another home, but . . ."

"Another home!" Fanny cried. "Why, she belongs right here with us, if those nice people say it's okay."

"It's more than okay," Wes said, with his eyes a little too bright. "And they know you'll give her a good home."

Fanny frowned. "Now where do you suppose I put that old sewing machine, sister? And all that pretty material. Oh, it will be so much fun makin' up a bunch of cute little pinafores, and maybe a few bows to go in her hair."

"That's fur," Frances admonished. She looked at Jennifer. "Or is it hair?"

Jennifer giggled. "It's hair. I'll have to give you a list of instructions, and you'll have to follow them. . . ."

Frances held the chimp close, and protectively. ''Don't imagine she can have any elixir, for one thing, and we'll have to make her up a bed. Well, the two of you just come on into the house, and we can have a long talk over a hot cup of tea and some of Fanny's pound cake.''

''Bananas,'' Fanny was saying. ''Monkeys like bananas.''

Frances snorted. ''She isn't a monkey, she's an ape, sister, and best you not hurt her feelings by calling her otherwise!''

Jennifer and Wes followed the sisters into the cottage, and Jennifer couldn't remember the last time she'd had such a warm, wonderful feeling. And the best part was knowing that a little bit of magic from the circus had been left behind in Calico after all.

''New beginnings around,'' Wes said softly.

''New beginnings filled with love,'' Jennifer murmured, taking his hand.